"Dallas, can I see your hand?" Zora pointed to his left hand, hanging at his side.

He looked at her strangely, but complied. That, apparently, was when he first saw it, too. "Is that a—"

"Wedding band?" Zora stepped closer on wobbly legs, barely able to get the words out of her mouth. "It is. And this—" Zora held up her hand and showed it to her friend "—appears to be its match."

Dallas's eyes widened and he slapped a palm over his gaping mouth for a moment.

"Dallas, these aren't cheap trinkets." She pointed to his ring. "I'm almost sure those are real diamonds set in platinum."

Her friend stared at his hand again, blinking, but not saying a word.

"My phone is charging now, but I need to check my credit cards. All of them. I have several bags in my room from a *bridal* shop. I think we honestly might've gotten—"

"Married." Dallas's voice was hoarse. He waved a piece of paper that he'd picked up off the dresser. "According to this document, we are now Mr. and Mrs. Dallas Matthew Hamilton."

* * *

*Waking Up Married* by Reese Ryan is part of The Bourbon Brothers series.

Dear Reader,

Welcome back to the fictional town of Magnolia Lake, Tennessee, where my Bourbon Brothers series is set. This series follows the romantic adventures of the Abbott siblings—four of whom help run the world-renowned King's Finest Distillery.

In *Waking Up Married*, Zora Abbott finds herself in a sticky situation when she awakes in Vegas married to her longtime platonic best friend—Dallas Hamilton. Zora is already labeled the impetuous hothead of the family, so it doesn't bode well for her bid to lead her family's company into the future. And in the midst of the deal of a lifetime, getting married under the influence won't do much for Dallas's reputation either. But when the best friends strike a deal to stay married for one year, they'll discover that there's more to their lifelong friendship than either of them has been willing to admit.

Thank you for joining me for the passion, secrets and drama of my Bourbon Brothers series. If you have a question or comment, visit reeseryan.com/desirereaders to drop me a line. While you're there, be sure to join my VIP Readers newsletter list for series news, reader giveaways and more.

Until our next adventure,

*Reese Ryan*

# REESE RYAN

---

# WAKING UP MARRIED

# HARLEQUIN®
## DESIRE™

Recycling programs
for this product may
not exist in your area.

ISBN-13: 978-1-335-23278-6

Waking Up Married

Copyright © 2021 by Roxanne Ravenel

This edition published by arrangement with Harlequin Books S.A.

For questions and comments about the quality of this book,
please contact us at CustomerService@Harlequin.com.

Harlequin Enterprises ULC
22 Adelaide St. West, 40th Floor
Toronto, Ontario M5H 4E3, Canada
www.Harlequin.com

**Printed in U.S.A.**

**Reese Ryan** writes sexy, emotional love stories served with a heaping side of family drama.

Reese is a native Ohioan with deep Tennessee roots. She endured many long, hot car trips to family reunions in Memphis via a tiny clown car loaded with cousins.

Connect with Reese via Facebook, Twitter, Instagram or reeseryan.com. Join her VIP Readers Lounge at bit.ly/VIPReadersLounge. Check out her YouTube show where she chats with fellow authors at bit.ly/ReeseRyanChannel.

### Books by Reese Ryan

### Harlequin Desire

### *The Bourbon Brothers*

*Savannah's Secret*
*The Billionaire's Legacy*
*Engaging the Enemy*
*A Reunion of Rivals*
*Waking Up Married*

### *Dynasties: Secrets of the A-List*

*Seduced by Second Chances*

Visit her Author Profile page at Harlequin.com, or reeseryan.com, for more titles.

You can find Reese Ryan on Facebook, along with other Harlequin Desire authors, at Facebook.com/harlequindesireauthors!

Thank you to all of my amazing readers and fellow authors who've read and helped promote my Bourbon Brothers series. Your enthusiasm for and willingness to recommend this series to fellow readers has meant so much to me.

To the phenomenal readers in my Reese Ryan VIP Readers Lounge on Facebook: y'all are the best! Thank you for your continued support, feedback and encouragement. I am forever grateful for it and for you.

# One

Zora Abbott sat in the nursery at her brother and sister-in-law's home, holding her new niece, who was barely a week old.

Remington Renee Abbott—Blake and Savannah's baby girl—was the newest addition to their growing family. And Zora was already obsessed.

Zora smoothed down her niece's headful of soft, shiny black curls as she stared into the girl's wide, dark, expressive eyes. She gently tapped Remi's adorable button nose. Baby girl blinked in response, her mouth opening slightly.

Remi stared at Zora as if she was both slightly amused and mildly disinterested at the same time.

Zora glanced over to where Savannah had suddenly appeared in the doorway. "Remi's facial expressions crack me up. She definitely has her mama's no-nonsense fierceness."

"And her aunt ZoZo's ability to look right through you and make you question yourself," Savannah added, smiling.

"True." Zora grinned. "You and Blake are going to have your hands full with this one."

"I don't doubt that," Savannah agreed. "And I hate to break up the lovefest, but your brother asked me to remind you that you need to leave for the airport soon or you'll miss your flight to Vegas."

"I know." Zora brushed the backs of her fingers against the baby's rosy cheeks. Remi's skin was the same soft brown as her mother's. "I just hate to be away from her for three whole days."

"Remi will be right here waiting for her aunt ZoZo when you get back." Savannah stepped into the room with its mauve-painted walls and straightened the dusty-rose bedding draped across Remi's crib.

Zora kissed her young niece's forehead, then reluctantly handed the baby to her mother. A hint of a smile ghosted over Remi's little face as her eyes lit up with recognition. Savannah cooed softly in the baby's ear, then nuzzled her forehead.

Zora bit back the envy that knotted her gut the tiniest bit. More than anything, she wanted children of her own. A startling realization she'd made nearly two and a half years ago—the moment she'd first held Remi's older brother, Davis. Zora had been sure it was a hormonal phase. A passing mood she'd get over once she'd had her fill of changing dirty diapers.

But the feeling hadn't passed.

Her desire to be a mother grew with each additional child born into their family. Davis. Her cousin Benji's twins, Beau and Bailey. Now Remi. Each wedding or baby shower she'd attended made her painfully aware of her deepening desire. Made her ache with a sense of loss over something she'd never even had.

The night after Remi was born, Zora had lain in bed, staring at the ceiling, preoccupied with her growing desire to be a mom. She'd climbed out of bed in the middle of the night, opened her laptop and researched the idea that'd been brewing in her brain for months.

Who said she needed to wait for Prince Charming to come along to become a mother?

Zora was the sales VP at their world-renowned family-owned distillery, King's Finest. Her family was among the wealthiest in the region. She certainly had the financial means to raise a child alone. And her grandfather, parents, brothers, and their significant others were all the village she'd need to raise a child.

She was days away from her thirty-second birthday. Why should she wait for some phantom husband who might never come along?

"Everything okay, Zo?" Savannah laid Remi down.

"Of course." Zora's cheeks burned, as if her sister-in-law had been privy to her thoughts. "Going over a few things in my head before the trip."

"Well, I'll go let your brother and nephew know you'll be ready to leave shortly." Savannah squeezed her arm. "That'll give you two a few more minutes."

Zora nodded at her sister-in-law gratefully, then returned her attention to her niece, whose heavy eyelids drooped as she drifted off to sleep.

She glided her fingertips over the signature burned into the wood of the crib. It was a gorgeous original piece, handcrafted by Zora's longtime best friend—

premier furniture maker Dallas Hamilton. The reason for her Las Vegas trip.

Dallas was being honored with an award for innovation, thanks to a stunning line of furniture he'd designed the previous year. He'd spent months in Thailand working with native furniture artists, studying their designs and learning their craft.

He'd designed breathtaking pieces that were a marriage of Western and Eastern aesthetics, inspired by intricate Thai designs. And the award-winning collection included pieces designed by native artists.

Zora couldn't be happier for her best friend.

The award presentation in Vegas capped a whirlwind year in which Dallas had graced the cover of high-profile magazines, been asked to design furniture pieces for a growing number of celebrities and done a handful of television interviews.

Since they were both currently single, he'd invited Zora to Vegas as his plus-one for the award ceremony. Afterward, they would spend their final forty-eight hours in Vegas partying—an early nod to her impending thirty-second birthday.

It was nothing unusual for them. Dallas had been her plus-one at countless weddings and business or family events. And whenever they were both single, which was far more often than she liked to admit, they vacationed together at least once a year.

Dal still owned the cabin his grandfather had left him years ago, complete with a workshop where he handcrafted pieces—like Remi's crib—or developed new designs. It was the workshop where his grandfather had taught him how to make furniture and cabinetry when he was just a little boy. Dallas still considered Magnolia Lake home, but he spent most of the year at various places around the world, opening new showrooms for his company, Hamilton Haus, teaching workshops and being inspired by the unique furniture designs of various cultures.

Zora tucked the soft blanket beneath her niece's chin and smoothed down her hair. "Goodbye, sweet pea. Auntie ZoZo will be back soon," she whispered to the sleeping newborn before slipping out of the room and quietly closing the door behind her.

Zora hated to leave her niece behind, but she was eager to see Dallas. She'd made an important decision, and she needed to ask a huge favor of him. Her stomach twisted in a knot when she imagined how he would react.

# Two

Dallas Hamilton stepped out of the beautiful glass shower at the luxury hotel where he'd been staying all week. The suite, comped by the organization honoring him with an award later that evening, was far more elegant than anything he would've booked for himself.

His furniture design company had done quite well since its humble beginnings in his grandfather's barn ten years ago. Still, growing up, his family hadn't had much. So though he'd learned to enjoy the money, he hadn't been able to forget how quickly a person's circumstances could change.

He could still remember the day his mother had sat him and his older brother down to tell them that she and their father were getting a divorce. And that they would be moving into their grandfather's house.

That memory never left him. It reminded him that

people and circumstances were temporary and to avoid
getting too attached. Which was why his lifelong friendship with Zora Abbott was a minor miracle.

Dallas secured the towel around his waist and wiped
the condensation from the ornate bathroom mirror. He
scratched his stubbled jaw and surveyed his reflection.

His mother would say he needed a haircut and a
shave, tasks he usually tackled himself. But this was
one of those rare occasions that merited a splurge. So
he'd booked an appointment for an obscenely overpriced
facial and haircut in the hotel's posh spa.

"That's a pretty fancy towel and everything, but I
think you can do better than that for tonight."

Dallas jerked his head in the direction of the voice
as familiar as his own. Even when they were at opposite ends of the world, Zora's voice was often the last
one he heard before drifting off to sleep.

"Wasn't expecting you for a few hours, Zo. Or I
would've closed the door." Startled by her surprise ap-
pearance, his heart was still racing. Dallas tightened
the towel around his waist, lest he end up flashing his
friend. His bare chest, on the other hand, Zora had seen
countless times on the beach or at the pool.

"I know." Her dark eyes glimmered, and one edge
of her mouth curved in a slow smile that honestly did
*things* to him that it shouldn't.

Because they were best friends. Nothing more. Despite that inadvertent-ish kiss beneath the mistletoe a
couple years ago that nearly derailed their friendship.

"I sent a text about switching my flight yesterday."

"Sorry, Zo. I didn't get your message."

He hated text messages and social media.

*Anything worth saying should be said in person, or at least on the phone.*

It was his grandfather's philosophy, which he'd happily adopted. Dallas used text messaging sparingly, out of deference to Zora, his older brother and the occasional girlfriend. But a good old-fashioned phone call was still his preferred method of communication.

"Sorry you had to make it here on your own. I'd scheduled a driver to pick you up at the airport."

"It's fine." A smile lit Zora's face, and her terra cotta–colored skin practically glowed beneath the bright bathroom lights. She stepped just inside the doorway and leaned her shoulder against the wall, her arms folded. The innocent gesture lifted her breasts and exposed more of her cleavage in the low-cut top.

Not that he was looking. He was observant, and he couldn't help noticing things.

Yep, that was why his eyes were drawn there, not because…

Dallas cleared his throat and scratched his chin, returning his attention to his own scraggly hair and face in the steamed mirror.

While most women he wasn't sleeping with would have probably taken the hint and retreated from the bathroom by now, his best friend wasn't shy. Nor was she big on privacy. Especially that of the men in her life, given that she'd grown up in a house with her father, Duke Abbott, and four older brothers.

She gripped her chin, her head cocked as she studied his face. As if they were sitting together fully clothed in the living room.

"I know, I know." Dallas ruffled his hair, which was a few inches longer than he usually wore it. "I need a haircut and a shave. My mother told me yesterday when we had a video call."

"Sounds like Tish," Zora laughed. She stepped closer and spiked her fingers through his wet hair, tugging it to its full length.

"The haircut I can't help you with," she said. "But I can definitely shave you. I've gotten good with a straight razor. Pops taught me how so I could shave him," she added when he cocked an eyebrow.

Pops was her grandfather, Joseph Abbott. Grandpa Joe was the Abbott family patriarch and the founder of the distillery that she, her siblings and her father now ran. He'd had a stroke several weeks ago. He was at her parents' house recovering and, according to Zora, driving all of them crazy while they looked after him.

"You're offering to shave me with a straight razor?" He guffawed. "Sounds like a setup to a really cheesy murder mystery, and I'm the guy who ends up on the floor with his throat slashed in the first five minutes of the film."

"Give me a little credit." Zora smirked, propping a fist on one generous hip. "If I planned to murder you, I'd be much more clever about it than *Oops, I s'pose the razor must've slipped clean out of my hand.*" She pressed the back of her other hand to her forehead in a dramatic pose.

Dallas chuckled, rubbing his chin. "I have no doubt you're right about that. But I think I'll pass on the shave just the same." He winked at her. "I have an appointment for a haircut and a shave in the spa downstairs."

"Ooh. Look at you being all fancy. You're not turning into one of those high-maintenance men, are you? Because there is only enough room for one high-maintenance personality in this relationship, and I think we both know that's me." She pressed her open palm to her chest.

"Don't worry, your spot is safe, Princess." Dallas grinned, invoking the nickname that Zora's father still sometimes called her. A nickname he knew his friend hated. She was always competing with her brothers. She didn't want to be a princess. She wanted to be king of the hill, especially as they all jockeyed to be named the successor to Duke Abbott as CEO of King's Finest.

"*Don't* call me princess." Zora punched him in the gut playfully.

"Fine." Dallas chuckled. "But I have to get dressed or I'll be late for my spa appointment. So you've got exactly five seconds to get out of here or I'm ripping off this towel." He gripped the towel in what they both knew to be an idle threat.

"Hmm…" Zora rested her chin on a closed fist. "Is that supposed to make me want to leave?"

"Get out, Zo." He pointed toward the door, trying his best to maintain a serious expression.

"All right, all right." She turned and begrudgingly left the bathroom, then made her way across the large, well-appointed master bedroom. "But I'm starving. I'll go downstairs with you to grab something to eat."

"Perfect. See you in five." He shut the bedroom door behind her and changed into jeans and a T-shirt.

He'd invited Zora to stay the weekend with him in Vegas because he had this large suite all to himself and her birthday was coming up soon. It seemed like the perfect opportunity for them to have an early birthday celebration in Sin City, since he had plans to spend most of the next month traveling between his factories in Europe and Asia.

Normally, they would have separate rooms on a trip like this. But the suite was huge and had two master bedrooms on opposite sides of the living space. He figured the place was big enough for the two of them to share without any awkward incidences.

Clearly, he'd been wrong.

Then again, the situation just now had only been awkward for him. Zora, who was as comfortable in her gorgeous brown skin as any human being he'd ever known, hadn't thought twice about the encounter. In fact, she probably couldn't fathom why he would.

Maybe a few years ago, he wouldn't have. But since their kiss…

Dallas sank onto the bed and ran his fingers through his wet, too-long hair.

Things had been…*different* between them since Zora had kissed him beneath the mistletoe at a charity ball he'd attended with her in Nashville one Christmas.

The kiss had caught him off guard. He honestly would've been less surprised if Santa and an army of elves had raided the place. So he'd frozen like a deer caught in the headlights; incapable of reacting.

She'd taken his delayed reaction as a rejection. But before he'd been able to tell her that he'd wanted to kiss her, too, Zora had blamed it on the alcohol and the moment. She'd apologized profusely and insisted that it would *never* happen again.

In the weeks following the kiss, Zora had avoided him. She wouldn't answer his calls and responded to his text messages with cryptic, one-word responses.

So he'd finally flown home from Thailand, gone to

her office and insisted that they hash it out. And they had. They'd agreed to pretend the kiss had never happened and never to cross the line again. Because neither of them wanted to jeopardize their friendship.

Only, a part of him wondered if maybe they *weren't* better off being just friends.

There was a tap at the door. "Dal, I'm starving. Are you dressed yet?" Zora sounded like a petulant child on a long car trip asking, *Are we there yet?*

"Yes, I'm dressed." Dallas grabbed a pair of socks from his bag.

That was all the invitation his friend needed. She entered the room. "Ready?"

He slipped on his other sock. "Almost."

"Okay." Zora's voice suddenly seemed small, and her expression turned serious.

Not the reaction he was expecting.

Dallas reached for the burnished brown leather Tom Ford sneakers Zora had gifted him last year to mark the opening of a Hamilton Haus showroom in London. "Everything good, Zo?"

His friend glanced down at her clasped hands before finally meeting his gaze again. "I know you have an appointment to get to, but could you spare ten minutes? I *really* need to talk to you about something."

"Of course." Dallas slipped on his shoes, then patted the space beside him on the bed. "Sit."

Zora sank onto the mattress, her denim-clad knee brushing against his. Her soft scent—a mixture of floral and citrus notes—tickled his nostrils. The warmth from her brown skin seemed to embrace him. His heart beat a little faster, and he willed other parts of his body to behave.

*She's your best friend. Mind out of the gutter, pal.*

It wasn't as if he hadn't sat beside Zora on his bed before—both as kids and adults. But not since their unexpected kiss.

Dallas swallowed hard, hoping that his friend wasn't about to utter the words he constantly feared. That this would be their last adventure together because she'd fallen in love with some guy who couldn't deal with their friendship.

"What is it that you want to talk to me about?" It alarmed him that Zora Abbott—who had never in her life been at a loss for words—suddenly seemed reluctant to say what was on her mind. He covered her hand, flattened on the bed between them, with his much larger one and squeezed. "You know you can talk to me about anything, right? This—" he used his free hand to gesture between them "—is a judgment-free zone. Always has been, always will be. So whatever you need to say or ask—"

"I want to have a baby," Zora said abruptly. The words rushed from her mouth like a torrent of water, suddenly unleashed. She turned to him, her eyes searching his, as if gauging his reaction. "Not down the road when the right guy comes along," she added. "I want to have a baby *now, Dallas.*"

He was sure his heart had stopped momentarily. After all these years of friendship, Zora Abbott had a gift for surprising him. But never more than right now.

"You want to have a baby?" Dallas stammered, feeling a little light-headed. His throat was dry, and his heart was trying its best to beat right out of his chest.

She nodded, staring at him expectantly. For the first

time in a long time, the invincible Zora Abbott seemed vulnerable.

There were few things in the world Dallas would refuse this woman. But was Zora really asking him to father her child?

# Three

Zora prided herself on being fearless. She had nerves of steel and wasn't easily intimidated. She'd stared down misogynistic liquor industry execs and vendors, never giving them a single inch of unearned ground.

But right now, Zora was filled with uncertainty and trepidation as she stared into her best friend's widened brown eyes. His warm beige skin had suddenly gone pale and his gaping mouth could catch flies. Dallas clutched her hand as tightly as he had whenever they went on some crazy roller coaster together, which he'd always ridden purely for her sake.

"You want…a baby?" Dallas repeated, his words stilted. "Now. With me?"

"Yes." She nodded—until his final words registered in her brain, as if on delay. "Wait…what? No, not *with* you, Dallas."

She tugged her hand from beneath his and stood, pacing the floor. What did he think this was? Some cheesy rom-com?

Dallas looked utterly confused and a little disappointed. He scratched the back of his head. "I thought you were asking—"

"For your support." She stood in front of him and folded her arms. "*Not* your DNA. After that kiss weirded you… I mean *us* out…the last thing I'd do is ask you to father my child."

God, it sounded so *real* when she said it aloud.

She was going to ask some random stranger to father her child. Well, not really random. Her baby's father would be screened and carefully selected for his mental acuity and promising gene pool. She'd make her selection rationally. Without mind-numbing emotions or messy attachments.

Zora expected Dallas to look relieved that she wasn't asking him for a sperm donation, but his frown deepened, and he looked more confused than ever. "You want to have a baby on your own?"

"If I could do this totally on my own, I'd be a mom already." She sank onto the mattress beside him again. "Obviously, I need a little help to make this happen."

"I'm aware of how babies are made, smart-ass." Dallas sounded only slightly irritated as he dragged a hand through his longish brown hair. "But if you're not asking me for…" Dallas's words trailed off and he cleared his throat. His forehead and cheeks flushed.

He was obviously uncomfortable with the idea of making a donation to the my-best-friend-wants-a-baby cause. She was glad she hadn't asked him for one.

The idea had certainly occurred to her. She'd known

Dallas most of his life. She'd known and loved his grandfather and adored his mother. Dallas was a good, kind, decent guy. No, scratch that. He was an amazing man. Funny and smart. Creative and generous. And they had a great relationship that had spanned decades with only the slightest hiccup: their ill-advised kiss a couple of years ago.

She'd been more than a little buzzed. And Buzzed Zora lacked the filter that reminded her of things like the impropriety of staring at her best friend's rather impressive biceps and pecs. Or his generous ass, which she was pretty sure you could bounce a quarter on. Or the way he sometimes licked his lower lip in a move that would make LL Cool J proud.

Sober Zora realized it was a normal, hormonal reaction for her to notice those things. To maybe even have the *slightest* physical reaction to them. But Sober Zora realized she shouldn't dwell on such thoughts. And under no circumstances whatsoever should she ever act on them.

Buzzed Zora obviously hadn't agreed.

So she'd kissed her friend, sending him into minor shock that night. There were a few seconds when she'd wondered if the man was still breathing.

Thankfully, Dallas valued their friendship enough that he wouldn't allow her to slink off into the sunset, dying of embarrassment. She hated to admit it, but the fiery speech her usually even-keeled friend had given her after flying halfway across the world to set things right only made him more attractive.

Zora groaned quietly, just thinking of it. Her mind and body had been at war then, just as they were now. She found comfort in the quiet assurance conveyed by the grip of his strong hand. But it stirred feelings she'd rather not have about her best friend, just as the kiss and its aftermath had.

Yes, of course, she would love it if Dallas Hamilton was the father of her child. But she valued their friendship too much to risk it with such a monumental, relationship-changing request.

Gauging Dallas's reaction, she made the right call.

"Me wanting to be a mom probably comes as a shock to you." She studied his face and those expressive, whiskey-brown eyes.

"I've seen how in love you are with Blake and Benji's kids. And Davis and the twins certainly adore you. And then the way you gushed over Remi when she was born..." Dallas gripped her hand again. "No, Zo, I'm not surprised. And I know that you're going to be an incredible mother."

"Thanks, Dal. That means a lot." Zora was moved by her friend's words.

"But as your friend, I have to ask...are you sure about this? Yes, I know you're more than capable of caring for a child on your own, and that you'd have a ton of support from your family. But are you sure you don't want to wait until you find the right guy? Rather than having some stranger's kid?"

Zora yanked her hand back. She wasn't angry with her friend for being honest about his reservations. She respected Dallas's willingness to say the things she needed to hear, even when she didn't want to hear them. Still, the phrase *some stranger's kid* hurt.

"It wouldn't just be some stranger's kid," she said. "It would be my child. And the father would have no legal rights to him or her. I would make sure of that," she said firmly. "And as for this dubious Prince Charming...

if he comes along, he would love me and my child…
regardless of who his father was. And there's no reason
we can't have a child of our own together. It's not like
I only want one."

"Sure. That makes sense, I guess." Dallas cleared his
throat and nodded, shoving his hands in his pockets.
"You've given this a lot of thought, it seems. So what
is it that you need from me?"

Zora stood, inching closer to him. "You're my best
friend, Dal. I need you to tell me that I'm not crazy for
wanting to do this. Especially now. While I'm competing with my brothers to be the next CEO of King's Finest. And I'd really appreciate it if you could be there
when I tell my family."

"Zora, you're one of the fiercest, most determined
people I've ever known." Dallas's eyes twinkled with
admiration. "You've never been afraid to tell your family anything. And you've never allowed anyone else's
opinion to sidetrack you once you're determined to do
something. Why is this different?"

Zora wasn't afraid of bucking the Abbott family tra-
ditions or of ruffling a few feathers. She had a lifetime
of practice doing both. But this was a monumental departure that would have long-lasting repercussions for
her and her child.

"I don't know." Zora shrugged. "It just is."

"I think you do know," Dallas prodded, his arms
folded.

He knew her too well. She did know; she just hadn't
wanted to say it. But Dallas clearly wouldn't be satis-
fied until she did.

Maybe she needed to say the words aloud.

"Because a part of me really wants my family's blessing and yours. I love and admire all of you. So it does matter to me what you all think. Especially about something as deeply personal as my child."

Admitting the truth made her feel as if a weight had been lifted from her shoulders. But it also strengthened her resolve. Zora tipped her chin up and met her friend's gaze, folding her arms, too.

"But I *am* doing this. Regardless of anyone's objections, yours or theirs. Still, it would mean the world to me if you all did support me," she conceded quietly.

The sound of her heartbeat filled her ears as she studied her friend's handsome face and thoughtful expression. Dallas wasn't rash or impetuous. And as much as she knew he cared for her, she also knew he wouldn't placate her. If he thought it was a terrible idea, he'd tell her so.

Dallas heaved a quiet sigh and tapped his chest twice with his closed fist—his silent show of support. Something they often did.

A sense of relief flooded Zora, and her eyes stung with tears. She returned the gesture, then leaped into her friend's arms. "Thank you, Dal. I can't tell you how much this means to me."

"Well, you know how much *you* mean to me, Zo," he whispered in her hair as he hugged her. "So whatever you need on this, I've got you. Just tell me where and when, and I'm there."

"I will." She grinned, relieved. "I promise."

He released her. "Now, c'mon. If I'm late, they're gonna charge me a ridiculous missed-appointment fee and give someone else my spot. Besides, if you plan to grow an entire human being, we need to make sure you stay healthy and well fed."

Zora nodded and slipped her hand into his as they made their way out of the suite and down to the hotel's main floor, where they parted ways.

Dallas hurried off to his spa appointment, and she followed the heavenly scent of savory grilled meat emanating from the hotel's bistro. But a lovely turquoise-and-pearl statement necklace in the window of a jewelry boutique caught her eye.

The necklace and matching earrings were beautiful. They would look lovely with the evening gown she'd selected for the night's festivities. A sales associate stepped outside the store, a broad smile on her face.

"Stunning, isn't it?" the woman said admiringly. "I've been waiting for the woman who could pull off that engagement ring, and it would be absolutely gorgeous on you."

"Engagement ring? No, I wasn't looking at the ring, I was looking at the—" Zora's attention shifted to the ring in the display window near the necklace.

She was speechless.

*Gorgeous* was an understatement. The ring had a large, heart-shaped, pink sapphire solitaire flanked by two sizable diamonds, also heart-shaped. And it was absolutely breathtaking. Zora cleared her throat. "Sorry, but I'm not in the market for an engagement ring. I am interested in that lovely necklace and the matching earrings."

"Oh. Sure. Of course." The woman's eyes dimmed. She maintained her smile but was unable to hide her disappointment. The difference in the commission on the two items would be vast. "Right this way."

Zora followed the salesclerk inside and tried on the necklace. As she stared in the mirror, she couldn't help wondering what Dallas would think of the piece. Which was silly. They weren't a couple; they were friends. *Just* friends.

But for the first time since she'd decided to have a child on her own, she felt a true sense of relief.

Everything would be fine. Because her best friend would be there to hold her hand through the hard part: telling her family.

# Four

Dallas stared in the mirror in his hotel bedroom as he retied his bow tie for the third time. He was much more of a T-shirt guy than a tux guy. Still, his mother had insisted that he learn to tie a bow tie rather than using a clip-on when he'd accompanied Zora to her first cotillion. In fact, nearly every time he'd worn a tuxedo, Zora Abbott had been on his arm for the occasion.

Either he'd served as her plus-one at some gala, charity ball or wedding, or she'd been his. Every time, he'd tied his own damn tie. So why did it seem that his brain and fingers had forgotten how to do it tonight?

Maybe it was because he was still in shock from Zora's news a few hours ago.

She wanted to have a baby.

Not some abstract child she'd have in the distant future with whomever she'd eventually fall in love with. She wanted to have this child now.

He'd spent most of the afternoon in a daze, going through the motions with Zora's words on his mind.

Mostly, he couldn't stop thinking of the few seconds when he'd mistakenly believed Zora was asking him to father her child. Despite the initial gut-wrenching shock he'd felt in that moment, the idea had been turning over in his head ever since.

Why couldn't he be the father of Zora's child? And rather than her going through some expensive laboratory procedure, why couldn't they just do things the old-fashioned way?

There was obviously an underlying attraction between them. And he and Zora knew each other better than anyone else. Wouldn't doing this with a friend be preferable to engaging the services of a stranger who might be lying about his Ivy League education?

Dallas huffed and undid the bow tie, which had turned into a disaster once again.

"Dal." There was the quiet rap of knuckles at the closed bedroom door. "I'm having a bit of a wardrobe issue. I could use your help."

Dallas opened the door. "What can I..."

The words died on his lips the moment he saw his best friend. Zora was always gorgeous. But today her beauty had ascended to a new level.

She was absolutely stunning.

Zora wore her dark brown hair, streaked with blond, in a partial updo. Part of her hair was swept into an elegant bun. The remainder of her natural curls were worn loose. Her dress was a vibrant pink perfectly suited to her skin tone.

The sleek column skirt of Zora's floor-length gown hugged her delicious curves. An overlay attached at the waist gave the magnificent dress an added flair of drama. The one-shoulder bodice of the dress revealed her shimmering brown skin with its red undertone, which seemed to deepen as his gaze drank her in.

"What?" Zora pressed a hand to her belly and glanced down at her dress. "You don't like it?"

"Are you kidding me? God, Zora." He was nearly breathless. "You look incredible."

"Thanks." She smiled, seemingly relieved. "You look pretty amazing yourself." She indicated his tuxedo. "Need help with that tie?"

"Please," he said. "For some reason I just can't seem to get the damn thing right tonight."

"It's just nerves." Her voice was soothing. "It's a big night for you and well-deserved."

Zora slipped the necklace in her hand onto her wrist before she began methodically tying the tie. A skill he knew she'd learned from her grandfather, well before he'd suffered his stroke.

"There." A bright smile lit her eyes. "Perfect."

"Thanks." Dallas tried to ignore the warmth of her body and her teasing scent. To focus his attention anywhere other than her pouty lips. And to drown out the voice in his head that mused about how sweet it would be to lean down and taste her mouth. "You needed something, right? What can I do for you?"

"Two things, actually. First—" She turned her back to him, revealing that her dress was only zipped halfway up. "If you wouldn't mind?"

"Of course not." Dallas zipped the dress, which fit Zora to a tee.

"And then if you'd help me with this clasp, I'd appreciate it." She handed the necklace to him, and he placed it around her neck and fastened it.

Zora thanked him and turned around, indicating the matching earrings. "Do I look good enough to be on the arm of tonight's guest of honor?"

"I have no doubt that you'll be the most beautiful woman in the room."

"Wow. You're swinging for the fence." Zora's eyes danced with amusement. "But it's sweet of you to say. I can always count on you for a boost of confidence." Zora patted his chest. "Ready?"

She turned to walk out of the room, but Dallas grasped her wrist stopping her. Zora turned back to him. "What is it, Dal?"

"I've been…that is, I was thinking that…" He was blabbering like a complete idiot.

She probably thought he'd already started drinking. Especially since he'd received several gift baskets that afternoon. Most overflowed with fruit, baked goods or coffee. But at least two of the gift baskets included various types of liquor. Including one he'd received from his older brother, Sam, with explicit instructions not to open it until after the award ceremony.

"What is it, Dal?" Zora asked again. This time she looked slightly alarmed. "You're not getting a little case of stage fright, are you? Because everything will be fine. Just watch where you're walking so you don't fall off the stage. And even if you did, it's not the end of the world."

"Not helpful," he said. "But no, I don't have stage fright. At least, not about tonight."

Zora folded her arms. "Okay, now I'm curious. What do you mean?"

"I mean…" He took a deep breath, still not believing the words he was about to say. "I understand why you didn't ask me to be the father of your baby."

"Because it would be complicated and messy and just plain weird…for us and our families," she quickly pointed out. "Besides, that's a big ask of a friend. Not the kind of thing you put on your birthday wishlist."

"It is a big ask," he acknowledged. "But being a mother is obviously very important to you, Zo. So helping you achieve motherhood is important to me. Besides, regardless of the circumstances, making a baby with someone…that's a lifelong connection. Wouldn't you prefer to make that kind of commitment with someone you're already friends for life with, as opposed to a random stranger?"

"I know we're in Vegas, but I'm not going to the sperm slot machines, Dal. There's a careful screening and selection process. I'll know who this man is. That he's the kind of person I'd want half of my child's DNA to come from." Zora looked slightly flustered. "And I'm feeling a bit judged here, which is something I thought I could count on you *not* to do."

"I'm not judging you, Zo." He lifted her chin, forcing her eyes to meet his. "I'm just saying I'm here, and I *want* to do this for you."

"And I love you for that, Dal." Her smile didn't quite reach her eyes. "But I won't jeopardize our friendship again. It means too much to me. So while I appreciate your offer, all I really need from you is your support. All right?"

He nodded, forcing a smile that probably didn't reach his eyes, either. "Fine. Whatever you need."

"Good." Her smile seemed more genuine now. "Now

hurry up. I'm hungry again. Plus, there's an open bar. Let's get there before the good stuff is gone."

Zora had a gift for injecting humor into even the direst situations. She'd done that when his grandfather had died five years ago, alleviating a pain that felt simply unbearable.

"You're hungry again? Sure you're not already pregnant?" Dallas chuckled.

"Watch it, sucka." Zora pointed at him, doing her best imitation of Esther from *Sanford & Son*. "Don't make me strangle you with that bow tie."

He held up his hands in surrender, laughing as he turned off the bedroom light and followed her into the living space.

Zora grabbed her clutch off the bar, eyeing one of the gift baskets wrapped in purple cellophane.

"That one right there has my name on it." She pointed to the basket. "There's coffee liqueur in there, and those brownies look decadent."

"Probably the reason Sam doesn't want us to eat them until *after* the awards ceremony." Dallas patted his stomach, laughing. "Personally, I've got my eyes on that bottle of vodka." He indicated a different basket.

"It's a date, then. After the ceremony tonight, we come back here, change into our pajamas and plan how we're going to celebrate my birthday for the next two days." Zora grinned, then cocked one eyebrow and smirked. "Unless, of course, you hook up with some pretty brunette. If so, be sure to leave a sock on the door, so I'll know."

"Smart-ass." Dallas raked his fingers through his freshly cut hair before extending an elbow to his friend. "C'mon, let's get you something to eat."

Zora slipped her arm through his, and they headed for the door.

He should be relieved Zora hadn't taken him up on his offer to be her baby's daddy. She was right. It would be complicated and messy. They'd have lots of explaining to do to their families.

He was a happy bachelor, content to have his friendship with Zora as the only long-term relationship in his life. Fathering her child would change that.

Dallas was *not* his father. If there was a child in this world who was half his, there was no way he wouldn't be in his or her life.

But at this rate, maybe he'd never be anyone's father.

Given the shitty relationship record of the men in the Hamilton family, maybe being an eternal bachelor was for the best.

# Five

"Okay, this one first." Zora brought the basket with the purple cellophane over for Dallas to open first. "Those fudge brownies and that coffee liqueur have been calling my name all night."

"Go ahead and open it. I'm working on my own basket here." Dallas ripped open the basket containing his favorite premium vodka and set the bottle on the bar.

The ceremony had been spectacular. The innovation award he received from such a prestigious organization was the highest honor of his career thus far. It meant a lot that his fellow designers had designated him for the award. He'd made some excellent industry connections and had a wonderful evening with the most stunning woman in the room on his arm. Plus, he'd managed to avoid tripping onto the stage for his acceptance speech.

*Total win.*

Zora's eyes lit up like a kid at Christmas. She carefully opened the basket, then unwrapped the brownies. She placed the bottle of coffee liqueur on the counter beside the vodka.

She took a bite of a brownie and moaned with pleasure. "*Oh. My. God.* Dallas, this brownie is a tiny slice of heaven. You *have* to try one."

"Seriously, Zo, no brownie is *that* good." Aside from a homemade pie, Dallas wasn't big on baked goods. But the sounds of indescribable pleasure his friend was making as she nibbled on the small square made him more than a little curious.

"I promise you, this one is. You have to try it." Zora broke off a piece and popped the morsel into his mouth.

He chewed slowly as he assessed the taste. It was rich and delicious. Filled with walnuts, and more like fudge than cake.

"Okay, you might be right about this thing," he acknowledged.

Zora finished hers, then picked up two of the other baskets she'd been eyeing. "Can we open these?"

"Absolutely." He grabbed two glasses from behind the little bar. "That's what they're here for."

Zora unwrapped the two baskets and removed the bottles of alcohol inside each one. She set a bottle of amaretto and a bottle of Irish cream liqueur on the counter beside the bottles of vodka and coffee liqueur.

She stood back and crossed her arms, her brows furrowed, as if she was in deep thought. Suddenly, her eyes lit up, and she snapped her fingers. Zora turned to him and grabbed his arms.

"I got it. You know what I could really go for tonight?" she asked, then excitedly answered her own question. "A screaming orgasm."

"You…wait…what now?" His throat went dry.

"A screaming orgasm," she repeated, one brow furrowed. "The cocktail."

He spiked a hand through his hair. "Never heard of it."

"It's something I had at a bridal shower once, and I loved it. It consists of vodka, Irish cream, coffee liqueur and amaretto." She pointed to each of the bottles in turn. "And I think I saw…" Zora rummaged through the already opened baskets, then triumphantly held up a small jar of maraschino cherries. "Aha! Now we just need to get room service to bring us up some milk and some whipped cream."

Honestly, he'd be happy with a beer or just a splash of his favorite vodka on the rocks. But they were celebrating his awards and her birthday.

So why not go all in?

"On it." Dallas called room service and ordered the missing ingredients. He could practically hear the person who took the order holding back a smirk. How often did the hotel get requests for a can of whipped cream?

Then again, maybe he'd rather not know.

Zora washed her hands in the small bar sink and rummaged through the cabinets. She found a half-ounce stainless steel jigger, a measuring glass and a mixing tumbler, then carefully poured measures of all four liquors into the cocktail shaker with the focus of a sci-fi villain working on a potion for world domination.

And though he tried mightily not to stare at the curve of her generous bottom in those cute little sleep shorts…well, he was her best friend, but he was also a man who had an extraordinary appreciation for a firm, well-rounded…

"You spent a lot of time chatting up the team from Iceland." Zora returned the last bottle to the counter and turned around.

Dallas's face flushed with heat. Had she caught him looking? If so, her expression gave no indication.

"Yes," he confirmed. "I mentioned a few months ago that they approached me about a possible collaboration. The owner of the company is very straitlaced and family-oriented. Believes in doing things the old-fashioned way. So he wanted to meet me in person before we move forward. They're a big, international player. So—"

"So this could be a *really* big deal for you. Not that you aren't already doing amazingly well," she quickly added, placing a hand on his forearm and smiling. "Because you've accomplished so much on your own already. You took a hobby your grandfather taught you as a kid and turned it into…*this*." Zora nodded toward the three awards lined up on the bar. "This past year, you've been *killing* it."

There was a knock at the door before he could answer. Dallas grabbed some bills off the nightstand in his bedroom for a tip. He retrieved the milk and whipped cream and brought them to his friend. Zora measured the milk and added it to the stainless steel cocktail shaker. She added a few ice cubes to each glass, then to the metal container before shaking it up.

Zora poured some of the creamy concoction in their glasses, topping each with some of the whipped cream and a cherry. She handed one of the glasses to him and then raised hers.

"Dallas Matthew Hamilton, I am so damn proud of

you. Your grandfather would be, too. I only wish he was here to see it himself," Zora said with a sad smile, her voice trembling slightly.

"I think he would be proud." Dallas agreed, trying to ignore the twisting in his gut. "I wish Grandad was here, too. But I'm really grateful that you are. I know you have a lot on your plate with King's Finest right now. So I appreciate you dropping everything to come out here for this. It meant a lot to have you beside me when they called my name tonight."

"Wouldn't have missed it for the world." Zora clinked her glass with his, and they both took a drink. "Mmm... this is good. A little stronger than I remembered," she noted. "But good."

"Agreed." Dallas took another sip. He was a coffee fiend, so he'd always enjoyed coffee-based cocktails. He picked up the coffee liqueur bottle and examined the label. "Wow, Zo. This stuff is ninety proof. Maybe you should take it easy on this."

"I sell alcoholic beverages for a living, Dal." Zora's laugh came out as more of a snort. "I can hold my liquor. Don't worry, I promise not to take advantage of you if it's a little too much for you." She winked and took another sip.

"Smart-ass." He grabbed another brownie from the box and bit into it. "*This* is a damn good brownie." Dallas waved it for emphasis before taking another bite. "You weren't exaggerating."

Zora picked up another square and nibbled.

"I told you," she muttered through a mouthful. "Remind me to thank Sam next time I see him."

Zora ran a hand through her hair, which she'd taken down the moment they returned to their hotel room. The dark curls with hints of blond dusted her bare shoulders, exposed by the tank top she wore with her adorable little sleep shorts.

Dallas gripped his glass and tried to ignore the fleeting image of him running his fingers through those curls. Something he hadn't dared to do since he'd tried it when Zora was in the fifth grade. She made it clear he best *never* run his hands through a Black woman's hair again unless he'd been given *explicit* permission.

"The drink is a winner, too." He sipped it. "But I don't know that it's screaming orgasm good." He chuckled. "That's a pretty high standard."

"It's definitely better than ninety-five percent of the orgasms I've had that weren't self-induced." Zora sipped her drink.

Dallas sucked in a deep breath, inhaling some of the liquid. He coughed and sputtered, reminding himself of how embarrassing it would be if he choked to death and died with a raging hard-on caused by visions of his friend and her self-induced orgasms.

"Are you okay?" Zora reached out to pat his back.

"Yes. A little of my drink just went down the wrong way." He held out a hand, keeping her at bay and hoping she hadn't noticed his body's reaction to her words. He sank onto the sofa and changed the subject. "We won't be able to travel the world together and hang out all night drinking once you're a mom."

He'd said it jokingly, but he was struck by the aching realization that it was true.

"This is the end of an era for us, Zo."

Did he look as pitiful as he suddenly felt?

Zora juggled her drink, the cocktail shaker and another brownie, bringing them over and setting everything on the coffee table. She folded one leg beneath her and sat beside him, her thigh brushing his.

"I'm not *abandoning* you, Dal." Zora snuggled beneath his arm, draped over the back of the sofa. "But we all grow up eventually, Peter Pan."

"One of us is." He sullenly sipped more of his drink. "You've got your eyes on the CEO position at King's Finest. Now you want to become a mom." He paused, considering how he should phrase his next statement. "I'm surprised you want to do this right now, while you're making a case to be the next CEO."

"No one thought for a single moment that Blake becoming a father would hinder his ability to lead the company." Zora said indignantly.

He'd definitely hit a sore spot. Understandably so. "I'm not saying that, Zo." He rubbed her shoulder. "It's just that being a CEO and being a mom are two huge, life-changing, time-consuming endeavors."

"And I'm one hell of a multitasker." Zora winked, setting her glass on the table with a clang. She nibbled on more of her brownie. "Besides, Dad doesn't plan to retire for another few years. So the timing is perfect."

He gave her a weak smile and finished off his glass. "Like I said, you've really thought this through."

"I have," she assured him. "I know I can sometimes be a bit hotheaded and impetuous. But I'm done with that. I'm making good choices and careful decisions. Proving to my father and grandfather that I'm more than capable of leading the company and continuing their legacy. So don't worry. Everything will be fine."

"All right." Dallas poured the remaining cocktail into their glasses before holding his up in a toast. "May you get everything you desire and more."

"May *we* get everything *we* desire and more." Zora clinked her glass with his.

*Not possible.*

She wanted to start a brand-new life as a mother and a busy CEO who wouldn't have time for him anymore, while he wanted more moments alone with her like this.

So he would make the most of the next forty-eight hours. Because it might be the last time the two of them ever got to spend time together like this.

# Six

Zora awoke to harsh sunlight spilling into the room. Which room and where she was, exactly, her brain didn't quite register. Her head was throbbing in response to the light filtering through her closed eyelids, so she had no desire to open them.

She sucked in a slow, deep breath, then cracked one eyelid open, followed reluctantly by the other. Her hair had fallen across her face and was blocking her vision. Which meant she probably looked a complete mess.

Zora swept the hair from her face and was greeted by sunlight gleaming off towering hotels on the Strip.

*Las Vegas.*

She was still in Vegas with Dallas. And she had some serious brain fog and one hell of a headache. Anything that had happened since the awards ceremony felt like a blur.

Zora honestly wasn't sure if she'd lost a few hours or a few days, which was disconcerting. Definitely not responsible, CEO/mom-in-the-making behavior.

She could already see her smug older brother Parker gloating about her being irresponsible and unworthy of running the company. Which meant she was never, *ever* telling him that she'd apparently drunk her weight in… God, she couldn't even remember what they'd been drinking.

Her head felt heavy, her tongue felt thick, she was too damned hot to be in an air-conditioned room and it felt like there was a weight around her middle. She needed coffee—lots of it—and an ibuprofen or four. And she wasn't sure what time it was, but she could do with a few more hours of sleep, too.

Suddenly, the bed shifted, and the weight around her abdomen tightened.

Zora screamed and tried to scramble away from the body invading her space and trying to spoon her. But in her inelegant attempt to create some space between her and her random hookup, she lost her balance and tumbled over the edge of the bed. Her limbs flailed, and her ass hit the carpet with a thud.

A thick ass and thighs apparently *did* save lives.

Someone should put *that* on a T-shirt.

Zora tried to spring up, but her wrist hurt when she put weight on it.

*Great.* She might've sprained her wrist, too. Well, maybe she only had one good wrist. But her legs worked just fine. So she was fully prepared to knee this dude in the family jewels if he didn't explain what he was doing in her bed.

*Pronto.*

The man suddenly shot up, as if he'd heard her scream on delay.

"Zora?"

"Dallas?"

They spoke simultaneously.

"What are you doing on the floor?"

"Why are you in my bed?"

Those words were spoken simultaneously, too.

"I'm not in your bed." Dallas winced, as if every word he uttered was reverberating around his skull. "This is my room."

She opened her mouth to object, but Dallas pointed to his army-green duffel bag on the floor, his favorite pair of cowboy boots leaning on the wall beside it. Zora glanced around the room. The two master bedrooms in the suite looked identical, except the furniture was oriented in opposite directions. Besides, none of her stuff was here.

Dallas was right; she was in his room and in his bed. Zora glanced down, suddenly aware of the cold air chilling her mostly naked flesh. She was clad in a pretty, lacy, strapless and backless off-white bodysuit, which she didn't recognize.

Zora's confusion turned to panic, and her face suddenly felt hot. She glanced up to where Dallas had extended his large hand to her.

Despite his wince, he looked handsome. And her eyes couldn't help following the smattering of light brown hair that trailed down his bare, broad chest and disappeared beneath the sheet pulled up to his waist.

Zora swallowed hard, then put her hand in his and allowed him to pull her to her feet.

"Nice…uh…bodysuit." Dallas yawned, then tipped

his chin toward the sheer, lacy garment that exposed more than a little of her hind parts.

"Very funny." Zora tugged at the sheet to wrap it around herself. She gasped when she uncovered her friend's morning wood—in all its naked glory. She quickly put the sheet back. "Dallas!" She shrieked. "Why aren't you wearing any clothes?"

"Again…my room." He gestured around the space. "I didn't realize I had company in my bed, but normally when I do, they don't mind that I sleep naked." He winked, then winced again, grabbing his head. "Ow."

"That's what you get." She folded her arms, then looked around the room. "Why am I in here and where are my clothes? Because, I assure you, this isn't mine." She pressed a hand to the fabric covering her belly.

"I kinda like it." He stretched, seemingly unconcerned about the disturbing situation in which they found themselves.

Dallas's laid-back demeanor was the perfect balance to her more…high-strung nature. Normally, she appreciated that about him and his ability to talk her off a ledge. He'd stopped her from doing a lot of ill-advised things over the years. But right now, when they had inexplicably shared a bed after a night of drinking and they were both in various states of undress, she wished her friend was experiencing at least a little of the panic that she was.

"I like this bodysuit, too," Zora said. "But that isn't the point. The point is that I didn't buy it, or at least I don't remember buying it." Zora pressed a hand to her throbbing forehead.

"It matches that." Dallas pointed to a garment thrown over a chair in the seating area by the window.

Zora walked over to the chair and picked up the back-less little white minidress—just the kind of garment that would go well with the bodysuit she was wearing. But this dress didn't belong to her, either.

Did it?

She held the glittering, sequined dress against her body. It certainly appeared to be her size, though the hemline was shorter than what she'd typically wore. Zora sniffed the fabric and recognized her perfume.

There was no doubt about the fact that she'd worn this dress. She only hoped she'd purchased both garments new.

"My credit card." She turned back to Dallas, who was yawning and running a hand through his hair. "If I bought these items, they'll be on one of my credit cards. I just need to check them. Where's my phone?"

They both looked around the room. Dallas's phone was on the nightstand. But her phone was nowhere to be found.

Had she lost it?

"I'm sure it's here somewhere. Maybe out in the great room or in your room." Dallas picked up his phone. "I'm calling your phone now."

They both got quiet as they listened for "Castle on the Hill" by Ed Sheeran—Dallas's custom ring on Zora's phone. She heard the faint sound of music.

"While you find your phone, I'm just gonna—"

"Get dressed?" Zora asked, hopefully. She'd already seen her incredibly hot friend in the buff once, and it was starting to tax her already suspect self-control. The last thing they needed was a repeat of that kiss or…worse.

"Yeah." Dallas spiked his fingers through his hair.

The muscles of his biceps bunched and flexed, as did his pecs.

Zora averted her eyes and whimpered quietly beneath her breath. Then she cleared her throat. "Awesome. Then we can talk about…whatever this was… over breakfast. I'm starving."

"Don't know if they'll still be serving breakfast." Dallas glanced at his phone again.

"Why? What time is it?"

"Almost two thirty," he said with a yawn.

"It's Vegas. I'm sure we can find someplace serving breakfast all day." Zora listened for the ringtone, but it had stopped. "Ring me again, please?" she asked.

Dallas nodded and yawned again.

Zora padded across to her room on the other side of the shared living space. She followed the sound of the music until she found her phone beneath a pile of clothing on her still-made bed.

Why had she taken out half the clothing in her luggage and strewn it all over her bed? At least that might explain why she'd purchased a new dress. Obviously, they'd done something for which nothing she'd brought seemed quite right.

Zora picked up her phone, which powered down in her hand. She groaned and plugged it into her charger. Then she glanced around the room for any sign of what had happened last night. There were several shopping bags in the corner.

Apparently, Buzzed Zora also enjoyed going on shopping sprees. Zora only hoped that her alter ego hadn't done too much damage to her credit cards and that everything she'd purchased—minus the killer bodysuit, which she *really* did like—was returnable.

Three of the bags bore the words *Bridal Shop* in fancy lettering. One was a garment bag, one contained an empty shoebox and another looked like the kind of bag that might be used for accessories.

Suddenly, it was hard to breathe. She dragged her hand through her hair, and a few strands of her tangled curls caught on her ring.

Ring? Zora squeezed her eyes shut, the hand stuck in her hair trembling.

She carefully unwound the strands that had tangled around the ring. With her eyes still shut, she sucked in a deep breath and pulled her hand from her hair.

*Please, no. Please, no. Please, no.*

She repeated the words in her head again and again, afraid to open her eyes and peek at the ring on her finger.

Zora slowly released a breath, then opened her eyes. She covered her mouth with her other hand to suppress the scream working its way up her throat.

She was wearing the pink sapphire engagement ring she'd admired in the jewelry shop the day before. The one the saleswoman had convinced her to try on.

The woman had been horribly wrong about there being no harm in dreaming. Because Zora was not only wearing the stunning pink sapphire and diamond engagement ring. She was also wearing a gorgeous diamond wedding band with alternating marquise and heart-shaped diamonds.

Zora clutched at her stomach, her hands shaking.

*What the hell happened last night?*

# Seven

Was it possible that she and Dallas had…no. They couldn't have. They *wouldn't* have. She was sure of it. Because while she might tend to be a bit impetuous, Dallas was a rock-solid, sensible guy who always appealed to logic. So there was no way they could've possibly…

Zora couldn't bring herself to say the words, not even in her head. But there was one way to find out.

She found her sleep shorts and tank top and threw them on before making her way back across the suite toward Dallas's room. She tapped on the open door.

"Dal, are you dressed?"

"Almost. Gimme a sec," he called back. "All right. C'mon in."

Zora stepped into the room, forcing herself not to babble in a panic. There was probably a perfectly logical explanation for all this. Maybe they'd gotten completely lit last night, decided to crash some themed costume party, and she'd gotten too carried away with the props. Or maybe…

Zora took a deep breath, her head spinning and her stomach tied in knots.

*Just calm down, Zora, and think.*

She could do that. Focus on her breath. Slowly breathe in and out. But first, she had to see her friend's hand.

"Dallas, could you…can I see your hand?"

He raised his right hand.

"No, the other one." Zora pointed to his left hand hanging at his side.

He looked at her strangely but complied, raising the hand in question. That, apparently, was when he first saw it, too.

"Shit. Is that a—"

"Wedding band?" Zora stepped closer on wobbly legs, barely able to get the words out of her mouth. "It is. And this—" Zora held up her hand and showed it to her friend "—appears to be its match."

Dallas's eyes widened, and he slapped a palm over his mouth. Then he held her hand in his as he compared the two rings side by side. His was a handsome ring with five sparkling square-cut diamonds set in a channel aligned across the center of the ring.

"Are these gag costume rings?" His gaze met hers. "I assumed that the tiara in the bathroom was part of some costume."

"There's a tiara in your bathroom?" Zora's voice squeaked.

She hurried into the bathroom and retrieved the sparkly tiara from the counter. It had weight to it, and the vine design was intricate and beautiful. Those were Swarovski crystals; she was nearly sure of it.

Zora returned to the bedroom, where Dallas stood near the dresser holding a sheet of paper, staring at it and then the ring on his finger.

"Dallas, this isn't some cheap trinket." She held up the tiara, then held out the hand bearing the engagement ring and wedding band. "Neither are these." She pointed to his ring. "And I'm almost sure those are real diamonds set in platinum."

Her friend stared at his hand again, blinking, but not saying a word.

"My phone is charging now, but I need to check my credit cards. All of them. I have several bags in my room from a *bridal* shop. I think we honestly might've gotten—"

"Married." Dallas's voice was hoarse. He waved a piece of paper that he'd picked up off the dresser. "According to this document, we are now Mr. and Mrs. Dallas Matthew Hamilton. Apparently, you've taken my last name. I honestly think that might be the most shocking part of all this."

"Let me see that." Zora took the paper from his hands and carefully read every single line. *Twice.* She handed it back to him and pressed a hand to her throbbing head. "No, no, no." She shook her head adamantly. "This isn't possible. We wouldn't do this. We wouldn't get…married." It was still difficult to say the word. "What would possess us to do this, and why the hell can't I remember any of it?"

Zora huffed, sinking onto the bed.

"Maybe this is just a bad dream," she said, more to herself than to him. "We'll wake up and everything will be just the way it was before we went to sleep. That has to be it."

Dallas pinched her arm, and she squealed. She slapped his hand.

"What did you do that for?"

"Just checking your dream theory." He grabbed a T-shirt out of his bag and tugged it over his head before sinking onto the bed beside her. "Besides, I doubt we'd both be sharing the same dream."

Zora groaned, dragging her hand through her hair, but being careful not to snag her ring on it this time. She turned to him. "What do you remember about last night?"

Dallas rubbed the back of his neck and sighed. "Not much." He shrugged. "I remember coming back here after the ceremony. We got in our pajamas for the night, and we were celebrating. You were making some drink with a whole lot of liquor in it. It had some crazy sex name."

"Right, I was making screaming orgasms," Zora said. "And then you told me that I should maybe slow down because the coffee liqueur was like a hundred proof or something. And we were stuffing our faces with those incredible little bite-size brownies your brother sent you. I know the drinks were kind of strong, and that would explain the killer hangover I have right now, but—"

"But maybe it wasn't the drinks or at least, not just the drinks." Dallas stood suddenly. "Are there any of those brownies left?" he asked.

"Are you really worried about snacks right now?" Zora asked.

"No, I just need to see the packaging." Dallas hurried into the other room with Zora on his heels. He rummaged through the baskets they'd opened last night until he found the one from his brother. He dug through its contents until he found the container. His head dropped and he groaned. "Well, that explains why Sam put a note on here not to open this basket until after the awards ceremony. These aren't *regular* brownies. They're edibles."

*Did he just say...*

"As in weed-baked-into-the-brownies edibles?" She walked closer, her arms folded.

"It appears so." Dallas handed Zora the packaging and took a seat on a nearby bar stool. "I'm sorry. I honestly had no idea my dumb brother would send me edibles in a gift basket."

Zora carefully read the label, something she wished she'd done the night before.

"This isn't your fault. You had no way of knowing. Besides, I opened the basket. I should've paid attention to the ingredients," Zora muttered, tossing the empty box back into the basket and sitting down on the stool beside her friend. "But remind me to strangle Sam the next time I see him. He owes us both an apology. And if I can't return all this stuff I bought last night, I'm going to be sending him a hefty bill. That ring alone was fifty grand."

"You're kidding." Dallas's eyes widened. He reached for her hand and studied the ring. Their matching rings gleamed. He nodded. "It's an incredible ring and it looks good on you."

"Too bad I can't keep it." She held her hand up and wriggled her fingers, admiring the way the light danced off the heart-shaped pink sapphire and the diamonds that flanked it. It was a truly lovely ring. And the color of the sapphire complemented her skin tone.

"Wait…you're assuming you purchased all this stuff," Dallas said. "But if, for whatever reason, we decided to get hitched last night, wouldn't I be the one buying the ring?"

"Traditionally, yes," she acknowledged. "But I can't imagine that you would've spent that kind of money for a ring. Let alone for a last-minute, drunken exchange of vows."

"You're saying I'm too cheap to have purchased that ring?" He frowned, pointing at her hand.

"No, I'm saying that you're frugal and sensible with your money." Zora squeezed her friend's shoulder. "It isn't an insult, Dal. I understand your insecurities around money," she said softly.

It wasn't something her friend liked to talk about very often, but she knew that he'd been traumatized by the sudden uprooting of his suburban life in a nuclear family in Nashville to live in the sticks with his grandfather in a run-down cabin. It had really shaken Dallas as a kid.

The sudden dissolution of his parents' marriage had done a hit job on his ability to trust and made him worry about money, even now that he had plenty of it. And though it wasn't something Dallas would ever admit, Zora was sure that it was part of the reason he always seemed to hitch himself to the wrong woman in the rare instances when he actually got seriously involved in a relationship.

He was afraid he'd be as shitty a husband and father as his own dad had been and still is. Douglas Hamilton was now working on his fourth marriage and second family. He and his much younger wife were expecting. Neither Dallas nor Sam were close to their father, though Sam did occasionally speak to the elder Hamilton.

"Again, not an accusation. Besides, we have bigger fish to fry. Like, going to the chapel listed on that piece of paper in there to find out if it's an actual, legal document. If it is, then we'll find out what we need to do to get it annulled."

"Great. I'm already following in the footsteps of my old man," he grumbled. "And I'm pretty sure this means I'll hold the family record for the shortest marriage in perpetuity."

"This doesn't count as a marriage. Both of us were obviously hallucinating or something. Shame on this cheesy chapel for marrying us in that state. The salesclerks should be ashamed of themselves, too." Zora propped a fist on her hip. "And it's not like we slept together…" She bit her lower lip. "I don't think."

"Believe me, Zo, if we had, you'd remember." Dallas smirked.

Zora couldn't help flashing back to the moment she'd pulled back the sheet earlier and discovered that her friend slept au naturel and that what he was working with was rather…*impressive.*

"I appreciate the big-dick energy, Dal—" Zora rolled her eyes when Dallas grinned "—but you're saying I'd remember…*that*…but not making the decision to *marry* you? Think about it." Zora shook her head. "And another thing—we're not going to tell anyone about this… *ever.* Like never, ever, ever. Not in this lifetime or the next. *Capisce?*"

"Fine."

Dallas had always kept his word to her. Still, his answer didn't sound very convincing.

"Pinkie swear?" She held up her pinkie finger.

"We're a little old for pinkie swears, Zo." Dallas tapped a finger on the counter of the bar. "But okay, fine. We don't tell anyone about the marriage—with the exception of our eventual spouses—and we get it annulled before we leave Vegas, if that's possible."

"God, I hope so." She hopped off the stool. "I need a shower and breakfast. Then we'll work all this out."

"I realize that the drunken marriage was a mistake, but you're not doing a lot for my self-esteem right now, Zo. Maybe tone down the I-can't-wait-to-get-rid-of-you thing just a tad." Dallas peeked through his thumb and forefinger.

"Sorry." Zora pressed a hand to her friend's cheek. "You're going to make someone an amazing husband one day. And she'll be incredibly lucky to have you."

"Just not you," he said solemnly.

"I…uh…" she stammered. *Is he serious?* Was he still hurt because she'd passed on his offer to be the father of her child?

"Because we're just friends. I get it. Give me fifteen minutes to shower. Then I'll be ready to go to breakfast." Dallas got up and walked away.

Zora hadn't meant to hurt Dallas's feelings. She was just being a little too honest. *Again.* She would work on that. *Really.*

Maybe she did have a lot more in common with Parker—who said just about every thought that entered his mind, completely unfiltered. Her brother was brilliant, but his people skills left a lot to be desired. Which was why she'd make a much better CEO than he would. She just needed to prove it to her father and grandfather.

A drunken, oops-we-made-a-mistake marriage? She might as well throw in the towel and admit that Parker had been right about her being an overemotional hothead who wasn't suited to run King's Finest.

Zora grabbed a bottle of water from the little fridge behind the bar and guzzled some of the liquid. She needed to stay hydrated and flush her system.

Hopefully, a hot shower and a fresh change of clothes would help clear her head. She needed to create a plan of action. Starting with packing up all the things that she'd purchased last night. Including that wedding dress that would've made her mother faint.

Duke and Iris Abbott would be horribly disappointed that their only daughter had gotten married in some Las Vegas chapel—probably by a jumpsuited Elvis impersonator with glued-on pork-chop sideburns. While wearing a tiara and a dress so short you could practically see her hoo-ha, as her mother would say.

Honestly, they were doing their families a favor by not telling them about their little Vegas adventure.

"Hey, Zo." Dallas was suddenly in the doorway of his bedroom, making his way toward her with his phone in his hand. "I'm pretty sure our deal not to tell anyone about our two-minute marriage is off."

"Why?" Zora set the bottle down and approached him. "Didn't we just agree it was best if they didn't find out?"

"That was before *this*." He handed her the phone.

There, in living color, was a video of the two of them, standing in a chapel. She was wearing the sequined minidress and tiara, and looking good, if she did say so herself. Dallas looked handsome in his tux, the same one he'd worn to the awards ceremony last night. They were in the middle of exchanging their vows during a surprisingly tasteful ceremony.

There was no Elvis impersonator—in a jumpsuit or otherwise. The chapel was tasteful and elegant. And neither of them behaved as if they were high off screaming orgasms and salted caramel brownie edibles. They just seemed…dreamily happy. She couldn't blame the officiant for believing they were simply a couple in love.

It was almost a shame that the ceremony wasn't real.

"So you took video." Zora shrugged, handing the phone back to him. "Erase it. What's the big deal?"

"The big deal is that I didn't take this video. You did. And you uploaded it to your Instagram account," he informed her.

"I *what*?" Suddenly, her head was throbbing again. She gulped down more water, then set the nearly empty bottle back on the counter. "I'll delete it. My family hardly pays attention to my IG account, anyway. It's not like I posted it to the company account."

"Look again." He handed the phone back to her.

Zora looked at the video. It was posted to the King's Finest Instagram account and it already had thousands of likes and hundreds of well-wishing comments.

*Shit.* Her parents were going to kill her. *If* they'd seen it. Maybe they still hadn't. She could delete the video, and maybe they'd be none the wiser. She just needed to get to her phone. Hopefully, it was charged up enough for her to access the app.

But then Dallas's phone rang, and the face that popped up on the screen was her mother's. She juggled the phone as if it had turned to hot lava in her hands, and Dallas caught it.

He looked at the screen. "Shit. If your mom is calling me—"

"She's seen the video, and she's already tried calling my phone."

Zora sank back onto the bed. Now her family knew about her ill-advised MUI—marriage under the influence. Zora slapped a palm against her forehead, then winced at the pain reverberating through her skull.

Any aspirations she had of climbing to the top of the ladder in her family's business were clearly toast. After a public screwup of this magnitude, she'd be lucky to hold on to the position she already had.

# Eight

Dallas stared at the phone ringing in his hand, still in a state of semishock.

He didn't do things like get drunk and get married. He was a laid-back, sensible guy. The one in the group who could always be counted on to appeal to reason. He'd talked his older brother out of breaking out the windows of an old abandoned farm when they were kids. And he'd convinced Zora not to take an ad out in a local newspaper declaring her ex a liar and a cheater.

So if he hadn't seen the video with his very own eyes, he honestly wouldn't have believed he was capable of this. In fact, he would've been more prone to accept Zora's joint dream theory or believed they were in *The Matrix* or some shit like that. Anything but the fact that he'd recklessly jeopardized Zora's chance to be named the future CEO of her family's distillery and sabotaged the deal he'd been working on for months with the Icelandic furniture company.

The stodgy, family-values CEO would not be amused when Dallas explained that he was as high as a fucking kite during his Instagram marriage to his best friend, which he was about to annul. So much for his trip to Iceland and the lucrative deal that would've gone along with it.

"I'm going to beat Sam's ass when I see him. He should have warned us about those brownies." Dallas huffed, thankful the phone had stopped ringing. He glanced over at Zora, sitting on the bed, looking stunned and miserable.

Just great. His descent into having the next broken marriage on his family tree was well on its way.

Dallas sighed and sat down beside Zora, draping an arm over her shoulder. "You okay, Zo? Can I get you some more water? Or maybe some coffee?"

"Belgian waffles topped with strawberries and whipped cream and a side of bacon," she said absently. "And I don't care what time it is."

"You've got it." Dallas squeezed his friend's shoulder and chuckled. "I don't care what I have to do, I'll make it happen. And I'll fix this. I promise."

"How, Dallas?" She turned to him, suddenly more lucid. "What on earth can we possibly do to fix this situation? We're screwed."

"I don't know," he admitted. "But give me an hour to think of something. I'll put my phone back on Do Not Disturb. You leave yours charging in your room. We'll go to breakfast and work this out, just like you said. All right?"

Zora frowned, then gave him a reluctant nod before getting up and making her way back to her room.

Dallas watched his friend walk away despondent, as if the weight of the entire world had come to rest on her narrow shoulders.

Seeing his fierce, confident friend looking broken and beaten gutted him. Especially since he shared the blame for what had happened last night.

Zora's mother called his phone again. Dallas groaned. He wasn't sure which scenario would break Iris's heart more—the prospect of him and Zora having *actually* eloped or the fact that their short-lived marriage had resulted from reckless behavior.

Unlike his train wreck relatives, to the Abbotts, family was *everything*. They all still lived in their little town of Magnolia Lake. They all worked together in their family-owned distillery, with the exception of Zora's older brother Cole, who had become the premiere home builder in the area. Most of them lived within a five-mile radius of each other. And they sat down to Sunday dinner at Duke and Iris's house nearly every week.

So he had no doubt that her parents would be heartbroken that their only daughter hadn't had a big, formal wedding, surrounded by friends and family with her father walking his baby girl down the aisle. And they'd probably be even more disappointed to discover that neither of them remembered what had happened. That it had all been a big mistake and they were about to get the marriage annulled.

"Zora!" Dallas hurried out of his room to the other side of the suite, hoping to catch his friend before she stepped into the shower.

She was standing by the bed in her room, neatly folding the clothing spread out on her bed and putting it into her luggage. The bridal shop bags were on the bed, too.

"Yes?" She looked up from her packing.

"You aren't leaving?" He felt a slight sense of panic at the prospect.

"No, I'm just repacking all the clothing I apparently tossed on the bed last night. Why? Did you think of something already?" Zora raised one brow doubtfully, then turned back to fold another blouse.

"No…well, yes…maybe." Dallas spiked his fingers through his hair, his heart racing.

"Okay, that couldn't be any less clear." Zora chuckled dryly. "Why don't you just tell me what it is that you're thinking, then we'll go from there?"

He felt like their roles had been reversed. That was usually the line he used on her.

Dallas took a deep breath before meeting her gaze. "I was thinking that… I mean…why don't we just…*not* get this thing annulled?"

"What?" His friend peered at him as if he'd sprung horns and a tail. "Your solution is that we *pretend* to be married? Why on earth would we do that?"

Not the response he was hoping for. But Dallas stood a little taller, prepared to make his case.

"First, it wouldn't be pretending, Mrs. Hamilton." He grinned, then jerked a thumb over his shoulder in the direction of his room. "We *are* married, and we've got the marriage license and video to prove it."

"I realize that *technically we are* married." Zora folded her arms. "But it's not like we intended to be."

"We might not remember intentionally getting married, but we obviously went through a lot of trouble to stage this wedding." He gestured toward the bridal shop bags on Zora's bed. "And I think I know why."

"This I'd love to hear." Zora sank onto the mattress. "Did you find that on your phone, too?"

"No." Dallas sat beside her, leaving some space between them. "But I offered to father your child, and I know you rejected the idea—" he added before she could repeat her objections "—but at some point we must've decided to do it. That's the only reason I can imagine that we would've done this. And since we already have—"

"Maybe you're right, Dallas." Zora shot to her feet and paced the floor. He tried not to be distracted by the tiny shorts she was wearing or the fact that he knew what she looked like in the lace bodysuit he could tell she was still wearing beneath it. "But all the reasons I had for objecting to the idea are still true. And now you're talking about what…forgoing the whole in vitro route and actually…" She halted her steps and looked over at him, her cheeks and chest suddenly flushed.

Not much made Zora Abbott blush. Obviously, the thought of the two of them *together* had. That gave him the smallest bit of hope that he could convince her.

"Have sex?" Dallas chuckled when Zora's eyes widened. "Yes, Zora, that's what I'm proposing."

"I appreciate that you want to help me, Dal. And you know that I love you as a friend." Her tone was apologetic. "I realize that I've chosen a non-traditional route to motherhood. But a small part of me wants to believe in the fairy tale. That one day the guy I'll fall head over heels in love with will come along. I don't want to settle for a partner because it's convenient. Not even one I care for as much as you. And as your friend, I want more than that for you, too. If we stayed married just so that you could do this for me…you'd come to resent me and our child."

Dallas walked over to her. "I could never resent you, Zora. You've been there for me, since we were kids. And you're the reason I have this business. You saw the vision long before I did. You encouraged me to take a leap of faith. And you backed me financially, even though I was determined not to take your money."

"I knew the investment would pay off." Zora shrugged, as if it were no big deal that she'd believed in him enough to arrange the financing for his start-up and invested a large chunk of her own savings in Hamilton Haus.

He'd paid every cent of it back, and then some. But the business could've easily gone down in flames. She'd stuck her neck out for him.

If Zora was truly opposed to the idea…fine. So be it. They'd have to deal with the consequences of last night's bender. But if she was turning down his offer because she was reluctant to accept his help, then he'd make it clear that he *wanted* to do this for her. Not out of a sense of indebtedness, but because she was his best friend, and he'd walk through a wall of fire for her.

"You stuck your neck out for me. Risked your reputation and your savings. So why is it so hard for you to let me do this for you?"

"I haven't been keeping a tally, Dallas," she said. "And I don't want you to do this to even the score or something. I had the means, so I helped someone I really care about. It's that simple," Zora said.

"Then let me do the same." He squeezed her hand. "Or are you getting cold feet about having a baby?"

"No." She shook her head. "I've never been surer about anything in my life."

"Then let me help you, Zo. Because I *want* to make this happen for you, not because I feel obligated to."

She studied his face, her eyes welling with unshed tears as she chewed on her lower lip.

He knew his friend well enough to recognize that she was actually considering his proposal.

# Nine

Zora took both of Dallas's hands in hers and met his gaze. Her friend had always been sweet, thoughtful, and considerate. And she'd always known that she could count on him for anything. But what he was now offering required sacrifice and long-term commitment.

She loved him all the more for it. But she needed to know that he'd really thought this through.

"Dallas, are you sure about this? Having a child together…we're talking about a lifetime commitment." She smiled. "That means you'll never truly be rid of me. Are you sure you're up for that?"

"I'm twenty-five years into this thing. No turning back now." He chuckled. "Besides, we were clearly going to outlive our spouses and become neighbors in one of those overpriced senior living centers where we'd play spades and dominoes all day, eat rice pudding, and complain about how our grandkids don't come to see us often enough." He shrugged. "We can still do that, only this way, we'll be talking about the same ungrateful grandchildren."

Zora burst into a fit of giggles, and Dallas laughed, too. But then an awkward silence filled the space between them.

Were they really considering doing this?

And if she was finding it awkward to have this conversation, how weird would it be when they actually decided to...*consummate* their marriage?

"There's one other thing." Zora's eyes drifted down to where their hands were connected. "I realize that we have a long history together, but as friends, not romantic partners. You're proposing that we actually have sex— for the sake of having a child," she added quickly. "But what if there's no—"

"Chemistry between us?" He chuckled quietly. "Maybe you've forgotten, but you kissed me a couple of years ago," he reminded her.

"That was also Buzzed Zora." A fresh wave of humiliation heated her cheeks, as she thought of Dallas's reaction to the kiss. "And that encounter didn't go so well, in case you've forgotten."

"I haven't." Dallas lowered his gaze and sighed. "That was completely my fault."

"No, it was mine. I tried to turn our friendship into something that it wasn't...that it *isn't*. And we'd be doing that again if we go through with this marriage."

"Because there's no attraction between us?" He raised one brow incredulously as he studied her face, his gaze lingering on her mouth.

Zora's heart raced, and she could feel her body reacting to the intense heat in Dallas's eyes.

This was new. Because Zora was reasonably sure
her friend had never looked at her this way before: like
he intended to devour her.

Dallas stared at his friend. Took pleasure in watching
a crimson streak spreading across her cheeks.

"I didn't say… I mean…when I kissed you, you
didn't…" Zora stammered, her espresso-brown eyes
suddenly wide.

Zora Abbott never hesitated. She laid down demands
with complete clarity. Was always clear about what she
did and didn't want.

In fact, there were few moments in his life when he'd
seen his opinionated friend truly speechless or even the
tiniest bit vulnerable. Something in his chest warmed
at being the reason Zora *Hamilton* stood in front of him
now thunderstruck, trembling and a little nervous. It
thrilled him that he had the power to give this incredibly strong woman pause.

Dallas leaned forward and took Zora's face in his
hands. He glided his thumbs along her cheekbones,
watching her eyes study his with anticipation as he
closed the space between them.

Finally, Dallas did the thing he'd regretted not doing
the night Zora had kissed him beneath the mistletoe.
He pressed his open mouth to hers.

Dallas's eyes drifted closed at the pillow-soft sensation of Zora's lush lips meeting his. He savored the
minty taste of her mouth, pushing his tongue between
her lips when she opened them on a soft gasp. He swept

his tongue over hers, then glided it along the ridges at the top of her mouth.

Zora wrapped her arms around him tentatively, her hands barely touching his back. As if she wasn't quite sure this was real. Slowly, she tightened her grip, her fingertips pressing into his skin through the soft cotton T-shirt. She leaned in closer, pinning his growing shaft between them.

An involuntary groan escaped Dallas's mouth at the sensation of his hardening length pressed to her soft belly. The feeling seemed to trigger awareness in every nerve ending in his body.

It opened the doors to the floodgates of desire for her that he'd long barred shut. Because Zora had always meant too much to him to risk their friendship for sex—no matter how badly he'd secretly craved her touch and her kiss. Now that it had been unleashed, his desire for her came stalking out of its dark, secret cave like a ravenous tiger in search of its prey.

His kiss became hungrier, more insistent than the tentative kiss he'd begun with, and Zora responded in kind. She gripped his shirt, her body cradled against his, as if she, too, ached for more contact.

Dallas dropped his hands to her waist, then cupped her full bottom. It was something he'd fantasized about much more than he'd care to admit. The fabric of her shorts filled his palms, but his fingertips brushed the exposed skin just beneath the curve of her perfect ass.

He gripped the firm flesh, squeezing it and pulling her closer. Intensifying the sensation that already rippled down his spine, overwhelming his senses with a need he'd never allowed himself to acknowledge because the stakes were simply too high.

Suddenly, his phone rang again, bringing them both out of the daze they'd fallen into as they stared in the direction of the ringing phone.

"Guess you didn't get around to turning the Do Not Disturb back on." She gave him a soft, playful grin that made him want to toss her onto the bed amid the luggage and bridal shop bags and kiss every inch of her smooth brown skin.

"Guess not." Dallas silently cursed himself for forgetting. He stroked her cheek, bringing her attention back to him. "Well, does that answer your question?"

"Yes, I think it does," she practically whispered, then sighed quietly, taking a step away from him. She cleared her throat, both of them ignoring his cell phone as it continued to ring. "And if you really want to do this, then I accept your offer of help. But first, we need to establish some rules."

*There* was the confident, take-charge woman that he knew. The one who always felt a need to be in control.

"Yes, Mrs. Hamilton?" Dallas smirked, maintaining his loose grip on her waist, even though she had put some space between them.

Zora frowned but didn't object to his use of her new last name. "We need to outline the parameters of this 'marriage.'" She used air quotes. "That way we both know what to expect. So I'm thinking that there's really only a window of five or six prime days for ovulation, so we'd only need to have sex then. I have a double master, so we can maintain separate bedrooms, just like we have here. Then we'd only need to come together… you know…when necessary."

She started pacing the floor, thinking aloud, as he'd

sometimes seen her do when working with her sales team at the distillery.

"Zora." He grabbed her arm gently. "I'm *not* your employee. I realize that the point of this exercise is to give you a child, but that doesn't mean that you're in charge of everything."

"Of course not." She frowned, clearly offended. But then she took a deep breath and released it. "I'm sorry if I gave you that impression. It's just that… I need things to be clear between us. And I don't want either of our feelings to end up being hurt. That's why it's best if we create an exit strategy *now*. So let's give this six months. Then we can tell our families we gave our marriage a try, but we're better off as friends."

"You really think six months is enough to convince our families that we gave this marriage our best effort?" Dallas asked, trying not to reveal his *already* hurt feelings.

Zora huffed, making her lips vibrate and her cheeks puff with air. "Right. We should make it at least a year. I mean…if you think you can maintain our sham marriage for that long," she said, her voice suddenly unsure. "I wouldn't blame you if you didn't. That's an awful long time for you to be off the market."

"Yes," he agreed. "We should plan to stay together for at least a year, but I submit that we should then reassess our feelings." His voice was firm as he maintained eye contact with her. "Because at the end of that year, maybe we'll discover that we don't want to go back to just being friends."

Zora inhaled sharply and blinked rapidly as she stared at him. "You're suggesting that we might want to make this a *real* marriage?"

"My one nonnegotiable condition for this agreement is that if we do this thing, it *will* be a real marriage. Same house. Same bed. Sure, we'll have sex during those optimal times, but also any time the mood strikes us."

"But—"

"Again, nonnegotiable." Dallas held up a hand, halting Zora midargument. "Nothing happens unless you want it to," he added for clarity. "But intimacy should never be off the table because of the calendar. Agreed?"

Zora tilted her head and folded her arms, resting her chin on one fist as she silently assessed him. As if she was seeing him in a totally new light.

He often allowed her to dictate when and how they spent their time together because, quite frankly, he didn't care what they did. All he cared about was spending time with her. But this was different. He loved his friend, but there was no way he was going to let her steamroll him on this agreement.

This was his opportunity to discover if there was something more between them than friendship. Something he'd often wondered about, especially since that kiss under the mistletoe.

"So you want to reserve the right to be spontaneous, but it's completely up to me?" she clarified.

"That pretty much sums it up." Dallas shrugged.

"Then I could only *want to* on those optimal dates," she pointed out with a smirk.

Whenever they negotiated anything, his best friend worked the hell out of that one year of law school she'd taken before she decided that she didn't want to be the King's Finest attorney after all. But then again, even as a kid, Zora had always been in active negotiation with the people in her life. She'd negotiated her allowance, chores, bedtime, curfew and the length of her skirts while in high school.

Dallas grasped Zora's tank top and tugged her closer, dropping another kiss on her soft lips. His tongue searched for hers. He wrapped his arms around her, kissing her until he'd elicited soft murmurs of contentment, and her hardened nipples poked against his chest.

He wanted more. But he wouldn't push. Wouldn't take her farther than she was prepared to go. This was only about making a point.

She wanted him, too.

Dallas broke their kiss, staring down at her as she finally opened her eyes. He grinned. "I guess we'll see about that, Mrs. Hamilton."

"Fine." Zora shoved him away, and he couldn't help laughing. "Point made, and your terms are acceptable. Do we need to write any of this down?"

She went back to folding her clothing on the bed.

"I think I've got it." Dallas winked.

His phone rang again. He recognized the ringtone as his mother's. Dallas sighed. "If we don't answer the phone—"

"I know, I know. They'll just keep calling." Zora huffed, then ran her fingers through her hair, fluffing it. "Let's just get this over with."

"But how do we explain our sudden decision to get married?" he asked.

"Let's keep things as nonspecific—but as close to the truth—as possible. You know…minus the weed brownies and the blackout," she added.

"Come here." Dallas grabbed his wife's hand and sat in one of the chairs in front of the wall of windows that offered a view of the Las Vegas Strip. He pulled Zora onto his lap, taking her by surprise. Dallas wrapped an arm around her waist, then handed her the phone. "Ready?"

Zora sucked in a deep breath, then nodded.

Let the newlywed games begin.

# Ten

Zora held her breath, her hands shaking as she sat on her friend's lap.

She'd shared tight spaces with Dallas plenty of times over the years. They'd shared tiny rental cars, a pop-up RV not much bigger than a soup can, and snug roller-coaster cars, to name a few. And they'd often sat close enough that she was *practically* on his lap. But *actually* sitting on Dallas's lap with his arm wrapped around her waist was a brand-new level of intimacy for them. One to which she would evidently need to become accustomed if they were going to pull off this temporary marriage of convenience for the next year.

But all this was a lot to take in.

Zora's head was swimming. Her heart was racing. Her body was overheating. Dallas's *impressive* man parts—the image of which she still couldn't get out of her head—poked against her bottom as he held her against him. Her lady parts were doing all manner of rogue things she'd much rather they not.

"You sure you're ready to do this?" Dallas asked.

The warmth and concern in his husky voice wrapped itself around her like a warm, soft blanket, assuring her everything would be all right.

"Yes. I'm ready." Zora sucked in a deep breath and slid her finger across the screen to answer the video call from Letitia Hamilton, whom everyone called Tish.

Zora and Dallas put on their biggest smiles.

"Hey, Ma." Dallas grinned.

"Hi, Tish." Zora waved awkwardly at the woman who'd gone from being her best friend's mom to her mother-in-law in an instant.

Tension suddenly knotted her stomach. She'd always gotten along so well with Dallas's mother.

Would she be angry with her?

"Iris, Duke, the kids finally answered the phone. I'm looking at them now," she called excitedly, not bothering to respond to either of them. Zora recognized the paintings in the background. Tish was in the family room at Zora's parents' house.

This could all go very bad fast.

Finally, Dallas's mother returned her attention to the screen.

"I can't believe you two went off and got hitched without telling us. And yes, I realize that I hate flying, but I would've driven across the country for my baby's wedding," Tish said. A hint of sadness altered the upbeat tone that she'd begun the conversation with.

"Or better yet, you could've gotten married right here

in Magnolia Lake so that we all could've been there."
Zora's mother's head popped into the edge of the frame.

Dallas tightened his grip around Zora's waist. She
took it as a silent reminder that they were in this together.

Zora sucked in a deep breath. She lifted her chin and
deepened her smile. "I know, Mom. And I'm sorry. Dallas and I honestly didn't come to Vegas with the intention of getting married."

"And when exactly did you decide that you two
were more than *just friends*?" her father asked from
off-screen, the tension evident in his voice.

"The realization hit us so quickly, sir. It's all kind
of a blur." Dallas jumped in when Zora didn't respond.

Oh, he was good.

"That's the only reason I didn't come to you first and
ask for her hand," Dallas said.

Zora pursed her lips and bit her tongue, forcing herself not to remind all of them that she was a grown-
ass woman who was nearly thirty-two years old. *She*
was the only person who could give her hand away in
marriage.

But since Tish looked sad, her mother seemed pissed
and her father sounded dejected…it didn't feel like the
best time to make her womanist speech. She put a pin
in it to save that conversation for another day.

Her father grunted his response and said that he was
going to the kitchen for a beer.

"I know your father is a little grumpy, but his feelings are hurt," her mother whispered loudly, squeezing
her face closer to the phone. "You're his only daughter,
Zora," she said, as if Zora wasn't well aware of that fact.
"He's spent your entire life dreading the day he'd finally

have to walk his baby girl down the aisle and give her away. But suddenly you're married, and he never got the chance to come to terms with it."

"I'm sorry, Iris," Dallas interjected, threading his fingers through Zora's and squeezing her hand, as if he sensed the tension knotting in her shoulders and back. "It's my fault. A whirlwind wedding here in Vegas was my idea. Once we realized how much we wanted to be together, we just got caught up in the emotions. We didn't want to waste another moment apart."

"Right." Zora glanced back at Dallas, flashing him a grateful smile. "Dal and I, we're both ready to settle down and start a family."

"So your father is right, you *are* pregnant." Her mother could barely restrain her excitement.

"No, Mom, I am *not* pregnant. I assure you," Zora said. "But Dallas and I are looking forward to becoming parents."

"That's so exciting." Tish beamed, sifting her manicured fingernails through her hair—the color of a brand-new, shiny copper penny. Her green eyes twinkled at the prospect. "And while you two haven't been answering the phone, hopefully working on making us those grandbabies," she added, causing Zora to stifle a cringe, "we've come up with a few surprise plans of our own."

*Uh-oh.* Zora did *not* like the sound of that.

"Um…okay." She glanced back at Dallas nervously. "What kind of plans?"

"We're going to have a formal wedding here at the barn. Nothing extravagant," Iris said quickly, before Zora had the chance to object. "Just a lovely little ceremony that both of our families can be a part of so your father can walk his little girl down the aisle, just like he always dreamed of doing."

"That sounds…really nice, Mom." Zora swallowed her objections. She hadn't intended to have the first wedding to Dallas. Now they were going to have a second, more formal one? "Right, Dal?"

"Sounds like a wonderful idea," he chimed in. "Thank you, Iris. Thanks, Mom. We can't wait to see you all when we get home."

*Home.* This still all seemed like some crazy dream she'd awaken from any minute now. But she and Dallas were married, and they were going to be living under a single roof as husband and wife for an entire year while they tried to make a baby.

"Zora—" Dallas squeezed her hand, bringing her out of her daze. "Your mother was saying how beautiful your rings are."

"Oh, thank you." She held up her left hand, showing off her new rings.

"My son has good taste." Tish grinned.

"He certainly does," Iris practically crowed. Then they both laughed.

"I couldn't agree more, Iris." Dallas grinned, his whiskey-brown eyes twinkling.

Zora sprang up from her friend's lap the moment she'd ended the call. She needed some space and a moment to clear her head.

"I'm going to finish straightening up this mess before the housekeeper comes in. Then I'm going to find out exactly how much damage I've done to my credit cards," she said. "I suggest you do the same."

He walked over to where she stood folding her clothing. "Are you sure you're okay, Zo? Hearing how disappointed your dad was about not getting to walk you down the aisle…that had to be hard."

"It was. And now they're planning to shell out real money for this wedding. I don't care what they just said. My mother is a Southern mama planning her only daughter's wedding. She's bound to get carried away. I can't let them waste money on an elaborate wedding for a marriage that isn't even real."

Dallas cupped her cheek. "I don't see the harm in giving them a chance to celebrate our marriage. But I'll do my best to make sure they don't get carried away."

"There is one other thing," Zora said.

"A prenup?" he asked.

"It's a little too late for that." A strike Parker would no doubt hold against her. "But before we start…you know…exchanging bodily fluids, we should both make sure that we have a clean bill of health."

"A fair point." Dallas chuckled. "I have no objections to that request. And since I have never had unprotected sex with anyone, I don't anticipate there will be a problem." He checked his phone, which was ringing again. "I need to take this call, do you mind?"

"No, but when you're done, can we grab something to eat?" Zora patted her belly. "I'm starving."

Dallas nodded and kissed her cheek, then answered his phone as he exited the room.

Zora sank onto the mattress and held up her left hand. She stared at her stunning new rings. The pink sapphire and diamonds sparkled in the sunlight.

A small part of her wished that all this was as real as Dallas seemed to want it to be. But they weren't two crazy kids in love who'd flown to Vegas to get married. She loved Dallas as a friend, and yes, there was an attraction between them. But they weren't *in* love. Settling for anything less would eventually leave one or both of them feeling resentful. It wasn't a risk she was willing to take with a friendship that meant so much to her.

This marriage wasn't about love or attraction. It was about making a baby. Once they did, they'd go back to being friends who also just happened to be co-parents.

It was the right decision for everyone involved.

# Eleven

Dallas stepped out of Zora's room, closing the door behind him. He cleared his throat and put on his brightest smile before accepting the call from the man he hoped to secure a deal with soon.

"Mr. Austarsson." Dallas made his way back to his room on the other side of the suite. "How are you, sir?"

"I am well, Dallas. Thank you." Einar Austarsson's thick Icelandic accent wrapped itself around every word he uttered. "But as I told you before, please call me Einar."

*Right.* Einar had made a point of explaining that in Iceland, they called each other by their first names—regardless of one's station.

"I am told by a member of my social media team that congratulations are in order for you and your beautiful new wife." The man chuckled with knowing laughter.

"Why did you not mention when you introduced her that the lovely Zora was your fiancée?"

*Because...she wasn't.*

"We wanted to surprise our families... *Einar*." Dallas made a mental effort not to call the man *sir*—a natural tendency as a man born and raised in the South.

"Well, I am sorry to disturb you on such a momentous day, but my plane leaves first thing in the morning. I thought it would be nice if you and I could sit down over a meal and discuss what a collaboration between our organizations might look like."

"I'd like that very much," Dallas said, grateful Zora had agreed to maintaining their marriage for at least a year. By that time, any agreement he and Einar came to should be signed and in progress. "My...wife and I were going to grab a bite to eat. But I could meet you right after that."

"How fortuitous!" the older man proclaimed. "Brigitta and I will join you. After our meal, perhaps our wives will excuse us to conduct our business?"

"I...uh...sounds great, Einar. Zora and I would love for you to join us," he said, hoping his new wife wouldn't mind.

Zora put on her brightest smile and greeted Einar Austarsson—a big man who towered over them wearing the warmest grin. He easily fit the bill of gentle giant.

Then she greeted his beautiful wife, Brigitta Wernersdóttir, who was the very definition of casual elegance. The stunning older woman wore a lovely, pale pink, cocktail-length chiffon dress with a sheer capelet that showed her upper back. And her makeup was flawless.

Zora had no doubt the woman awoke every day looking picture-perfect and put together. The very opposite of how Zora had looked when she literally rolled out of bed this afternoon.

Though she and Dallas had only been awake for a few hours, it was now early evening and she was still exhausted. Her mouth was dry and her head still hurt. Though thanks to an over-the-counter painkiller, it no longer felt like an African drum circle was being conducted inside her skull.

Still, she felt like roadkill, compounded by the trauma of discovering that—*Quelle surprise!*—she was now her best friend's wife. This was definitely not the way she'd intended to spend her pre-birthday weekend in Vegas. Nor was it what she had planned to be doing right now.

She'd been looking forward to a plate of Belgian waffles, dressed with fresh strawberries, doused in strawberry syrup, topped with a pile of fresh whipped cream and sprinkled with powdered sugar. And she'd intended on eating her decadent breakfast-for-dinner at some tacky, all-day buffet where she could wear a scroungy pair of leggings, a T-shirt, her darkest shades and a visor pulled down over her face.

But when Dallas had come to her and explained that Einar wanted to join them for dinner at the hotel's four-star restaurant… Well, how could she say no to playing the happy newlywed for the sake of his deal?

If she'd said no, Dallas would've understood. He wouldn't have complained or guilted her. And even if they hadn't been married, she would've done anything she could to help her friend nail this deal with the Icelandic furniture designer.

Still, the fact that she felt she *owed* Dallas because of the sacrifice he was making for her unnerved her. That was the feeling of obligation Zora didn't like hanging over her head. That made her chest feel tight and her skin itchy. She didn't like feeling beholden to anyone. As if she hadn't earned everything that she'd achieved in her life—despite her last name or the fact that she'd been born into a life of privilege.

Every day at King's Finest, she'd worked hard to prove that she was there because she deserved to be. As much as her father or any of her brothers. She realized that it was a personal hang-up that she needed to get over. And yet, in the back of her head, there was always the need to prove herself. To demonstrate to her grandfather, father and brothers that she'd earned her spot on that executive board.

Whenever she met with distributors and vendors, she carried a tiny chip on her shoulder. She was always prepared to put in check any man who made the mistake of believing she was just another pretty face. Or that she'd only been given the job because she was the granddaughter of Joseph Abbott, the founder of King's Finest Distillery.

But Zora was equally burdened with the concern that she'd come off as an angry Black woman for speaking her mind, doing her job, doing it well and not standing for any bullshit—as any male executive would be lauded for doing. So she'd learned to find that perfect balance between being a pretty face and the baddest bitch in the room.

So here she was, playing the part of devoted wife in full makeup, a fancy dress and heels that made her legs look amazing but pinched her toes. And she'd have to settle for a steak or some fancy pasta dish, which would probably be lovely—just not what she wanted.

Then again, she wasn't really playing a role. She was Dallas's wife now. A fact that still felt surreal. And she was his devoted friend who honestly would do just about anything to see this venture and his business succeed.

But tomorrow, Dallas owed her waffles.

The couples exchanged the requisite pleasantries until the hostess led them through the elegant restaurant to their table. Dallas pulled out Zora's chair and sat beside her, draping his arm over the back of it. His heat surrounded her, warming her skin—and *other* places. And his subtle scent tickled her nostrils, reminding her of how it had felt when he'd taken her in his arms and kissed her senseless—twice. When she'd momentarily forgotten that she and Dallas were just friends.

"How did you two meet?" Brigitta asked, smiling at them the way people often smiled at newlyweds.

Zora felt guilty for evoking such genuine emotions when their marriage had been the result of too-strong drinks and her failure to read the label on a brownie wrapper. Still, she smiled gratefully.

"We've known each other forever," Zora said. Her heart swelled and an involuntary smile curved her mouth, thinking of the day they'd first met. "In fact, we met on the playground in kindergarten, and we've been friends ever since."

"My wife is being too kind." Dallas chuckled, squeezing her shoulder. "I'd just moved to the area, and I was the new, shy kid in school. A couple of bullies tried to shake me down on the playground. Zora here, who was about half their size, blew in like a tornado, told both them off and promised that if they ever messed with me again, she'd sic all four of her older brothers on them. Needless to say, I never had a problem with them again, and she and I have been friends ever since."

Einar laughed so hard his forehead and cheeks turned bright red.

Brigitta pressed a hand to her chest and smiled. "That is the sweetest story I've ever heard."

"I'm pretty sure that was the day I fell in love with Zo." Dallas glided his hand lower, circling her waist and pulling her closer as he leaned in and kissed her cheek. "In retrospect, I'm surprised it took us so long to figure out that we were meant to be together."

Zora's cheeks flamed at the sweet, intimate gesture and the words—rooted in the truth—which felt so authentic. They were simply playing a role. The happy newlyweds. She realized that. But what he was saying and how his words affected her…it all felt so *real*.

When her eyes met his, Dallas had the most sincere smile. Her heart leaped in her chest, and her pulse raced. For a moment, she'd almost forgotten that Einar and Brigitta were sitting just across the table watching them like goldfish in a bowl. Oohing and ahhing like they'd just seen a baby take its first steps.

Fortunately, the server came and took their orders before she did something crazy, like climb on his lap and kiss him as though they were in their suite alone.

She ordered a seafood pasta dish, Dallas ordered a steak and Einar and Brigitta both ordered lobster. When the server walked away, Dallas excused himself to go to the restroom, leaving Zora alone with the couple momentarily.

"I know you're still newlyweds," Brigitta practically cooed, "but it is just so wonderful to see a young man so very much in love with his wife. And you two have such an advantage, having been close friends for so long."

"Thank you, Brigitta." Zora smiled. "My sister-in-law always teased that we were like an old married couple. So I guess there's not much we don't know about each other." Zora sipped her water.

"But have you ever lived together?" Einar asked. When she shook her head, he and his wife both chuckled. "Believe me, Zora. No matter how well you know a person, you never *really* know them until you have to live with them. But I'm confident that you two will manage the adjustment."

It was something she hadn't considered before. She'd lived with all her brothers growing up. She was closest to Cole—her youngest brother. But when Cole had moved in with her for three months while he was renovating one of his homes several years ago, she'd been ready to strangle him by the time he'd moved out. So there was definitely some truth to Einar's words.

Dallas returned to the table and put his napkin on his lap. "What did I miss?"

"We were just talking about how different it is actually living with someone." Brigitta smiled warmly. "Speaking of which…will you two be moving into your home in Magnolia Lake, Dallas? Or yours, Zora? Or are you buying a new place altogether?"

"Mine," Zora said quickly.

Her eyes met Dallas's as she slid her hand into his beneath the table and threaded their fingers. He hadn't objected to moving into her place when she'd suggested it earlier. He'd only stipulated that they reside in the same house and sleep in the same bed. As their eyes met now, seated in such close proximity, with his large hand wrapped around hers, the thought of sharing a bed with Dallas sent an unexpected shiver down her spine. Made her body tingle in places she didn't want it to, especially not here and now.

"Right, but we might revisit the topic once we have kids." Dallas cringed the moment he'd uttered the words, as if he hadn't intended to say them.

"You're planning a family already. How lovely." Brigitta seemed thrilled by the news. "You're such a sweet couple. You'll be wonderful parents."

"I'll do my best. But I know that Zora will be a phenomenal mother, because she's an amazing aunt and an incredible woman." Dallas lifted her hand to his mouth and brushed a kiss across her knuckles. His action evoked another *aww* from Brigitta and made Zora swoon.

Einar shifted the conversation to business, and Zora and Brigitta talked about some of the shows Brigitta and her husband had seen while they were in Vegas and the Broadway shows she hoped to see next time they were in New York City.

The server brought out Einar's and Brigitta's lobster and Dallas's steak. But instead of the seafood pasta Zora had ordered, the server set a plate of large, fluffy Belgian waffles with strawberries and whipped cream and a side of bacon in front of her.

"My waffles." Zora pressed a hand to her chest. It was an elegant restaurant, and this was an important business deal. So she hadn't inquired about whether she could order an off-menu breakfast item for dinner, but apparently Dallas had.

"I promised you waffles." He winked, picking up his knife and fork.

She kissed his cheek, which made Einar and Brigitta smile approvingly.

Had her best friend always been so thoughtful and romantic, and she just hadn't noticed? Or maybe she was just caught up in the fantasy that they were spinning for the benefit of the man Dallas hoped to do business with.

*This isn't real.*

Zora repeated the words in her head over and over again. At this rate, she'd be repeating them to herself a lot.

# Twelve

Dallas could barely contain his grin as Zora held court, telling Einar and Brigitta an animated, sidesplittingly funny story about their adventures in Peru when they'd climbed Machu Picchu together. They'd been just out of college and determined to see the world but woefully ill prepared for the climb.

While he and Einar had sketched out some ideas for their proposed collaboration, Zora and Brigitta chatted like two old friends, trading stories and sharing laughs. Brigitta had shown Zora photos of the couple's four children, and Zora had shown off photos of Davis, Remi, Beau and Bailey. They lingered over the meal, chatting for nearly two hours.

Dallas was surprised the busy restaurant hadn't asked them to vacate their prime table.

Finally, Einar stood and declared that it was getting late. They had an early flight and needed to retire.

"It's been a pleasure to get to know you and your lovely wife." Einar beamed as he took Brigitta's hand. "I look forward to working with you in the future."

"Same here." Dallas shook the man's hand firmly, then his wife's. "Have a safe flight back."

"Zora, dear, it was such a pleasure to meet you. I'll email you that information about mentoring women for executive positions. You'd be perfect for it." Brigitta hugged her. "Congratulations again on your marriage. I know you two will be very happy together."

"Thank you." Dallas slipped an arm around Zora's waist, and she leaned into him, her hand pressed to his chest. He kissed her temple, his heart swelling for reasons he couldn't explain. "I'm confident we will."

He took Zora's hand in his, threading their fingers as they followed the older couple out of the restaurant, bade them farewell and headed toward the elevator.

They stood in the elevator car alone, her hand still firmly in his. He no longer had reason to hold Zora's hand. So why couldn't he let it go?

"We were in such a hurry to leave the suite, I didn't get the chance to tell you how beautiful you look tonight, Zo." Without thought, his gaze dropped to the neckline of the off-the-shoulder wrap dress Zora was wearing. The rust-colored fabric highlighted the reddish undertone of her skin.

"Thanks." She fiddled with the ends of the belt at her waist. Her cheeks had turned crimson again.

Dallas was starting to enjoy his newfound superpower: the ability to make the unflappable Zora Abbott blush.

They rode the elevator up in silence. When they got off, they were still holding hands.

"You were a star tonight, Zora," Dallas said as they made their way toward their suite. "My designs and awards brought Einar Austarsson to the table, but I'm pretty sure you sold him on working with me. You made me sound like a philanthropist design genius."

"Because you are." Zora stopped and turned to him. "And thank you for making the special request for my waffles. I didn't think eating breakfast for dinner at a fancy restaurant would be a good look for your big, important meeting. That's why I didn't ask for them myself."

"It's what you wanted." Dallas shrugged. "And I promised to make it happen."

"I appreciate it," she said. "After everything that's happened today, I needed the comfort of my favorite breakfast meal. I know that sounds silly."

"It doesn't, and it isn't. I understand," he assured her as they stood in front of the door to their suite.

Dallas was reluctant to release Zora's hand. To separate himself from the warmth and comfort of the connection he felt with their palms pressed together and their fingers entwined.

In fact, what he wanted more than anything was to lean down and capture her mouth in a kiss again. This time, with no hesitation or interruptions. And he wouldn't stop with just a kiss. That was just the beginning of where he wanted to take things with her.

But they'd agreed to wait until they'd both had medical exams and he'd put Zora in the driver's seat. So he would honor their agreement, no matter how badly he wanted to take her to bed.

When he didn't make a move to retrieve the key card in his wallet, Zora waved her small purse in front of the card reader. The tumblers in the lock clicked, and the indicator light switched to green.

Dallas squeezed the handle, holding the door open for Zora. Once they were inside their suite, he slid off his suit jacket and toed off his shoes, eager to get into a T-shirt and a pair of shorts.

Zora kicked off her heels, then stooped to pick them up. "I'm going to get out of this dress and makeup. And I'm still exhausted. Would you be insulted if I turned in early tonight?"

"No, of course not. We've been through a lot today. Turning in early sounds like a great idea. I should do the same." Dallas hoped he'd managed to hide the disappointment he felt at the idea of going to their separate rooms. "Good night, Zora."

She nodded, then made her way to her room, closing the door behind her with a soft click.

Dallas got out of the shower, toweled off and pulled on the sweat shorts he'd brought to sleep in. The ones he'd started out wearing the night after the awards but had shed *after* his marriage to Zora.

It was still relatively early for a night in Vegas, but it had been an eventful twenty-four hours, and he was exhausted.

Dallas yawned and padded across the darkened room toward the comfortable bed that beckoned him. When he turned on the bedside lamp so that he could charge his phone, he was startled by movement.

"Zora?" Dallas ran a hand over his head. "I thought you were—"

"Same house, same bed. That was the deal, right?" she murmured, shielding her eyes from the light. "I, too, am a person of my word. Besides, I might as well get used to your snoring."

Dallas broke into laughter. He plugged the charger into his phone. "I do *not* snore," he countered. "I just breathe heavily. And you're on my side of the bed. Scoot over."

"Fine. *Anything* as long as you'll turn off that light. My head hasn't completely recovered."

Dallas turned off the light and climbed into the bed beside Zora, occupying the space that still retained her body heat. The pillow bore her signature scent. He lay on his back for a few minutes, staring at the ceiling before he finally turned on his side, his back toward her. "'Night, Zo."

There was a silent pause, and he wondered if she'd already fallen asleep. Finally, she said, "Sweet dreams, Dallas."

Dallas lay awake long after Zora had fallen asleep. A deep sense of longing filled his chest as he tried to keep his desire for his best friend at bay.

He was lying in bed beside the woman whose friendship meant more to him than just about anything in the world. But clearly, he felt something more than friendship for her, too.

Dallas closed his eyes and groaned. The words of his jackass brother—with whom he'd spoken earlier and had shown zero remorse over the situation—still floated in his head.

*Dude, you finally made your move on Zora. You're welcome. Now...do not fuck this up.*

If only things were that simple.

# Thirteen

Zora held her breath as Dallas turned onto the road that ran past the renovated barn where her mother was planning to hold their formal wedding. At the end was her parents' vast property and the home Cole had built for them.

Dallas had a tight grip on the wheel of his tricked-out GMC Sierra Denali pickup truck—one of the few luxuries her friend, who was now her husband, had splurged on. She could feel the tension rolling off his broad shoulders, too.

Still, he placed a hand over hers on the center console and squeezed it, offering her a confident smile.

Dallas pulled his truck into the driveway of her parents' home, already filled with the vehicles of her four brothers.

"Awesome. The entire motley crew is here," Zora muttered beneath her breath.

"If we stick to the plan, everything will be fine." Dallas pulled his hand away long enough to shift the gear into Park and turn off the engine. He squeezed her hand again reassuringly. "But I realize that this first day will be...uncomfortable. Believe me, I don't relish the idea of deceiving our families any more than you do. So if you'd prefer to just come clean and explain what really happened... I understand."

"No." Zora shook her head vehemently. In her head, she could already hear all the things that her parents and siblings would say. They'd use words like *reckless* and *irresponsible*. None of which described the future CEO of their company. "We came up with this plan for a good reason, and we should stick to it. For both our sakes. I'm a little nervous, but you're right. It'll be fine."

Dallas gave her a small smile, then nodded before hopping out of the truck. He went around to the other side of the vehicle to open her door.

Zora didn't move. Instead, she tugged on the bottom of her sweatshirt. Then she repositioned the scarf she'd draped around her neck to give her low-key look a bit of pizzazz.

She'd thrown on practically the first thing she'd seen when she and Dallas had arrived from Vegas and gone to her place to take quick showers and change their clothing. And now she was rethinking everything... including her outfit.

What did a person wear to a birthday dinner that had turned into a sorry-we-got-married-without-you party? She was pretty sure an old sweatshirt, distressed jeans, a pair of Timbs, and lip gloss wasn't it.

"You look beautiful, Zo. Stop overthinking it." Dallas's husky voice was as soft and comforting as the oversize sweatshirt she was wearing.

He was blowing smoke. Still, she couldn't help smiling. Zora ran a hand over her hair, slicked back and pulled tight into a low bun.

"That, sir, is a pity compliment."

He grinned, leaning in closer. His lips brushed her ear when he spoke. "You'd look amazing if all you were wearing was a potato sack, a pair of earrings and that heart-stopping smile of yours."

He stepped back and extended his hand.

"Thank you." Zora practically whispered the words as she accepted his offered hand. She stepped down onto the sideboard of the truck, then hopped onto the ground.

Dallas shut the door, then held her by the waist, pinning her in place as he gazed down at her. "Maybe we're still a little fuzzy on the details of our decision to get married," he said. "But we're staying married because you are a strong, confident woman who knows what you want." He stroked her cheek and smiled. "Don't let anyone get inside your head and make you lose sight of that. Not even the people you love."

Zora nodded, grateful for the pep talk. Dallas always knew what to say to talk her down off the ledge. And she loved him for it. She lifted onto her toes and kissed his cheek, one hand pressed firmly to his chest. "Thanks, Dal. For everything."

"For you, Zora?" He grinned. "Anything."

It was something he'd always said. She'd always taken it as sarcasm. Yes, she'd known that she could count on Dallas, and had suspected that he would've done her nearly any favor—even one as big as fathering her child. But she hadn't asked because she didn't want to take advantage of their friendship.

Over the past two days, Dallas had shown her that their friendship ran far deeper than she'd imagined. Reminded her how truly special it was. Confirmed that it was something she never, ever wanted to lose.

Those weren't just sarcastic words that Dallas had uttered. He meant them. And he was proving that here and now. She stared into the depths of his brown eyes, her hand still pressed to his chest.

If this "marriage" ruined their friendship, she would never forgive herself.

"You two planning on coming inside or are you just gonna make out with my sister out here for another fifteen minutes?" Cole stood on the front porch, his arms folded over his chest.

*Here we go.*

Zora grabbed Dallas's hand and threaded her fingers through his before turning in her brother's direction.

"*Really*, Cole? You're going all whiny-ass man baby on me right now?" Zora retorted as she and Dallas made their way toward the large porch of her parents' beautiful home.

"Nothing personal, sis." Cole huffed. "Some of us are hungry."

"Well, I suggest you eat a Snickers or something." Zora released Dallas's hand so she could hug her brother, despite the fact that Cole was being an asshole.

"Or you could just get your ass in here so we could eat." Cole chuckled when Zora playfully punched him in the gut. "By the way, happy birthday, little sis."

Her brother turned his attention to Dallas, the humor suddenly gone from his voice. "Dallas."

"Cole." Dallas nodded at her brother, his expression pleasant but unsmiling. He hadn't missed Cole's passive-aggressive swipe at him, and he was making it clear that he wouldn't be intimidated.

And damn if that didn't make her usually easygoing friend even hotter.

Zora slipped her hand into Dallas's again, and they followed her brother into the house. "Easy, tiger," she whispered. "Save a little of that big-dick energy. There'll be enough out-of-control testosterone in this house as it is."

He squeezed her hand but didn't respond otherwise. Dallas seemed to have his game face on, ready for whatever her brothers would throw his way.

Honestly, Zora was a little hurt and surprised by Cole's reaction. They were the closest out of the five siblings. Cole was the Abbott voted most likely to buck the system. After all, he was the only one of them who didn't work for the distillery. He'd taken a lot of heat for that, but she'd defended him vehemently to her brother Max, her father and her grandfather.

So she was more than a little irritated that Cole seemed pissed about her surprise marriage. He hadn't bothered to congratulate her and her new husband— a man he had always considered a friend. Zora took a deep breath and tried to put herself in her brothers' position. If one of them had secretly eloped and she'd had to learn about it from a social media post, wouldn't she be angry and hurt, too?

So she would try to maintain a cool head and keep that in mind while she dealt with whatever attitude they threw her way.

"Zora! Dallas!" Their mothers approached them as they came into the entryway of the house.

The space was decorated with mylar balloons in silver, hot pink, and black—her favorite colors. A *Happy Birthday, Zora* banner hung over the curved entrance to the dining room.

Her mother looked gorgeous in a dress with a festive, autumn-themed print. Iris Abbott's black hair, which hung to her shoulders in soft curls, was overcast with a burgundy rinse that camouflaged the few gray hairs she did constant battle with.

"I honestly don't know whether I should hug you or spank you both." Iris was smiling, but her eyes were misty. "You two gave us quite a shock."

Zora's mother hugged her, and Zora was relieved to sink into the comfort of her mother's warm embrace. "Sorry, Mom," she whispered into her mother's hair.

"I know, baby." Her mother squeezed her cheek as she studied her face. She glanced toward the living room, where her father and brothers and their significant others waited. "I know what it's like to be that much *in love*." She said the words in a teasing, singsong voice. "That kind of passion tends to get in the way of our better judgment. I was disappointed not to be invited to my only daughter's wedding, of course." Her mother sighed. "But I'm also very happy that you and Dallas *finally* figured out what Tish and I have known all along. You two were meant to be together."

Iris's smile deepened when she looked over at Tish, who was admiring Dallas's ring. Her new mother-in-law's green eyes locked with hers, and Zora froze, her stomach clenching in a knot.

Zora had always gotten along so well with Tish. Dallas's mother had often said that Zora was the daughter she never had. But that was when she and Dallas were just friends. Would she feel the same now that Zora had actually married her son?

After all, Cole had always had a warm and cordial relationship with Dallas. But in an instant, her brother's attitude toward the man who was now her husband had shifted.

Zora sucked in a deep breath as she mustered the strength to greet Tish and apologize for leaving the woman out of such an important moment in her son's life. But before Zora could utter a single word, Tish wrapped her arms around her and held her tight.

She'd received several hugs from Letitia Hamilton in the twenty-five-plus years that she'd known the woman. But never one as warm and lingering as the bear hug she was giving her now. Zora felt a sense of relief, but also a heightened sense of guilt for robbing Tish of a moment that must've been incredibly important to her.

"Zora, honey, I am thrilled that you're officially part of our family now. For so long, I've worried about my baby. That he would marry someone who wasn't right for him. Someone who could never make him happy." Tish pulled back and gazed at Zora, her eyes filled with tears as she cradled Zora's face. "I can't tell you how relieved I am to know that if anything ever happened to me, Dallas won't be alone. That he'll be with someone who loves him as much as I do."

"Thank you, Tish." Zora forced a smile, her voice trembling slightly. She'd been mentally preparing herself for negative pushback from their parents and older brothers. She hadn't expected such a genuinely warm and sweet reaction from Tish. "It means so much to hear you say that."

Zora's eyes welled with unexpected tears. Partly in reaction to Tish welcoming her into their family. Partly because she couldn't help imagining how devastated Dallas's mom would be when they ended their marriage one year from now. Zora hadn't considered how important it must be to the woman that her sons didn't make the same type of disastrous match Tish had made when she'd married Dallas's father.

"I'm sorry you all couldn't be there," Zora repeated.

As far as their families were concerned, she and Dallas had made the conscious decision to exclude them from their wedding. Then they'd had the *audacity* to share their happy nuptials with complete strangers on the internet. And just for good measure, she'd posted it all on the King's Finest Instagram account.

No wonder Cole was being such a dick about this. They all believed she'd been a selfish, bratty princess, and she had no defense to convince them otherwise.

Her family was hurt that they hadn't been there. Hell, in a way, she and Dallas hadn't even been there. Not in any real way she could process at the moment.

"You two will make it up to us with this wedding we're planning," Zora's mother interjected, one hand propped on her hip. "In fact, I have some dates I want to run by you two."

"Can the wedding planning at least wait until *after* we've had dinner?" Zora's father appeared in the doorway, his arms folded.

Zora could see the pain and disappointment on his face. Her chest ached, and her gut wrenched.

Dallas gave her hand a quick squeeze. Then they walked toward her father.

"Hey, Dad," Zora said, her voice tentative.

She was a grown woman who was in complete control of her own life. She held an important position in their organization, where she had to make tough decisions every single day. But as she stood before her father now, she felt like Daddy's little girl. And she'd disappointed her father. Hurt him, even.

Zora and her father didn't always see eye to eye. But he'd respected her decisions because she'd been woman enough to come to him and tell him exactly what she intended to do and why, even when she knew he wouldn't approve. But this whirlwind marriage made her feel every bit the selfish brat her older brothers sometimes teasingly called her.

"Hello, Dallas. Happy birthday, Zora. Glad you two made it home safely," her father said calmly. "They're all waiting for you in the other room. Your mothers made sure your brothers didn't ambush you. Mostly because they wanted to ambush you themselves."

Iris and Tish glared at him.

"Thanks, Dad." Zora stepped closer to her father. "And I'm sorry. I—"

"Come here, sweetheart." Duke opened his arms.

Zora wrapped her arms around her dad, her cheek pressed to his chest as she inhaled the scent of his familiar aftershave.

"You don't owe any of us an apology. This is about dealing with our expectations for your life. And that's our problem, not yours. Your brothers might be a little miffed, but they'll get over it."

Her father patted her back, then extended a hand to Dallas, who gratefully shook it.

"Thank you for understanding," Dallas said. He took Zora's hand once her father released her. "We'd better head in there."

Zora was relieved by her parents' reactions, but she now braced herself for the backlash from her brothers.

"Zora! Dallas! Congratulations!" They were practically tackled by Savannah and Max's girlfriend, Quinn. She'd grown close to both women and considered them close friends.

"And look who's excited to see her auntie ZoZo." Savannah grinned, rocking baby Remi in her arms and nodding toward her nephew Davis, who was bouncing in his booster seat at the table, a wide grin on his face.

"Hey there, handsome. I missed you." Zora tickled her nephew's tummy and kissed his cheek. "Were you good for Mommy and Daddy while I was gone?"

The little boy nodded, enthusiastically. "I help Mommy take care of Remi."

"Good job, li'l man." Zora tweaked the boy's nose. Then she kissed her sleeping niece's forehead. She turned back to look at Dallas. "Isn't she gorgeous?"

"She's beautiful." He nodded, a soft smile curving the edge of his mouth as he slipped an arm around her waist. Dallas gently stroked the baby's arm. "Congrats to you and Blake on the sweet little addition to your family."

An involuntary smile crept across Zora's face and her heart swelled. She recognized that look in her husband's eyes.

*He's imagining what our daughter will look like.*

It was something Zora had often mused about as

she studied Remi's sweet little face and stroked her soft curls.

Zora's heart melted. Until now, she hadn't considered that maybe Dallas was looking forward to parenthood, too. She'd believed he was only really doing this for her. But his warm gaze and genuine smile as he studied the sleeping newborn gave her a sense of hope that this arrangement would be mutually beneficial for them.

"No pressure, of course," Savannah said. "But maybe one day soon you two will have a little one of your own."

Dallas's smile almost looked shy. He nodded. "We hope so."

"Yes," Zora chimed in. "We definitely want kids... soon."

Kayleigh—her brother Parker's fiancée—came out of the kitchen with a glass in her hand. She smiled broadly, coming over to greet them.

"Congrats, you two. Happy birthday, Zora." Kayleigh gave them both a quick hug before she made her way to her seat beside sourpuss Parker.

Her brother's expression was dripping with the same condemnation he'd leveled at Zora when he'd implied that she was too emotional and irrational to lead the company.

Zora's free hand curled into a fist at her side as she stared her brother down. "Parker," Zora said, her tone daring him to say something out of line.

"Zora, Dallas." Parker's tone was measured. Kayleigh nudged her fiancé, not so subtly. He cleared his throat, then walked over to them. "Congratulations are in order, I suppose."

Parker extended a hand to Dallas, and her husband

shook it tentatively, as if he was waiting for the other shoe to drop.

Zora didn't blame him. Without even trying, Parker had a way of putting his foot in his mouth and pissing people off. Even when he honestly believed he was being helpful.

"Thanks, Park. That means a lot." Dallas patted her brother's shoulder.

Parker stared at Zora strangely for a moment. He pushed his glasses up on the bridge of his nose. Then he did the thing Zora hadn't seen coming. He stepped forward and...*hugged* her.

Parker definitely wasn't a hugger. So Zora appreciated the effort, no matter how pained it was.

Zora returned the hug, and she could barely hold back a smirk as Parker gave her back an awkward pat, as if he were petting Kayleigh's dog, Cricket.

*At least he's trying.*

Which was more than she could say for her other three brothers, whom she'd have choice words for when she had a chance to speak to them alone. She was honestly angrier on Dallas's behalf than her own.

The Hamiltons had been friends to the Abbott family for nearly as long as Zora could remember. They'd been there for most of their birthday celebrations, holidays and more Sunday dinners than she could count. So the fact that her brothers were acting brand-new because she and Dallas had chosen to get married made her increasingly hurt and angry.

She was about to read all three of them—telling them exactly what she thought of their standoffishness—when Dallas wrapped an arm around her again.

The intimate embrace seemed to relieve a little of the tension in her back and neck.

"It's okay, Zora. We expected this, right?" he whispered in her ear. "Don't let them get to you. Their feelings are understandably hurt. Just give it a little time and this will all blow over."

Dallas kissed her temple.

Zora leaned into him and released a quiet sigh. She nodded as the agitation simmering in her chest slowly died down.

She and Dallas took their seats at the table.

"Blake. Max." She casually greeted her brothers, as if it were no big deal that they were obviously angry with her, and Dallas did the same.

Savannah and Quinn shot their respective partners a look of disappointment. Each of her brothers responded with his own brand of a *What did I do?* facial expression.

"Now that our entire family is here—" Zora's mother beamed "—your dad has a few words he'd like to say."

Her father stepped in the room and stood beside her mom, taking her hand in his.

"First, happy birthday, baby girl." Her father smiled and everyone around the table echoed his birthday salutation, for which she thanked them.

"Now, I know Dallas and Zora's sudden marriage came as a shock to all of us and that we're all feeling some kind of way about it—whether we're hurt or angry or a little of both," her father continued. "But let's not forget that your sister is a sensible adult, fully capable of making her own decisions, whether we agree with them or not. We need to respect that. Just as she's respected and supported the decisions that each and every one of you has made." Her father looked at her brothers in turn.

"And as for Dallas…" Duke turned toward him. "You've always been an honorary part of this family. You're a kind, respectable, hardworking man. The kind of man I always hoped my daughter would marry." Her father smiled warmly, his voice breaking slightly. He cleared his throat and nodded in Dallas's direction. "Iris and I are sincerely happy to welcome you as an official member of our family, son."

"Thank you, sir." Dallas nodded, obviously moved by her father's welcome speech.

Zora got up and hugged her father again. "Thanks, Dad," she whispered to him.

She was grateful her father had set the tone for her older brothers, even if her mother had likely put him up to it.

"Where's Grandad?" Zora asked. Her grandfather had had a stroke a few weeks before Remi was born. His recovery was coming along well, but he often pushed it, determined to recover more quickly. Zora couldn't help worrying about him.

"Grandpa Joe was a little tired today. He had an early meal and lay down for a nap. Hopefully, he'll join us later. But I don't want to wake him. He needs his rest." Her mother took her seat at one end of the table, while her father took a seat at the opposite end. "Now, are we ready to eat?"

"Yes!" Everyone at the table, including Zora and Dallas, nearly shouted in unison. They all laughed, and it seemed to ease the tension a little.

Things got slightly less awkward as the night went

# FREE BOOKS GIVEAWAY

GET UP TO FOUR FREE BOOKS
& TWO FREE GIFTS
WORTH OVER $20!

*We pay for everything!*

# YOU pick your books –
# WE pay for everything.

**You get up to FOUR New Books and TWO Mystery Gifts...absolutely FREE**

Dear Reader,

I am writing to announce the launch of a huge **FREE BOOK GIVEAWAY**... and to let you know that YOU are entitled to choose up to FOUR fantastic books that WE pay for.

Try **Harlequin® Desire** books featuring the worlds of the American elite with juicy plot twists, delicious sensuality and intriguing scandal.

Try **Harlequin Presents® Larger-Print** books featuring the glamourous lives of royals and billionaires in a world of exotic locations, where passion knows no bounds.

## Or TRY BOTH!

In return, we ask just one favor: Would you please participate in our brief Reader Survey? We'd love to hear from you.

This FREE BOOKS GIVEAWAY means that we pay for *everything!* We'll even cover the shipping, and no purchase is necessary, now or later. So please return your survey today. You'll get **Two Free Books** and **Two Mystery Gifts** from each series to try, altogether worth over **$20!**

Sincerely

*Pam Powers*

Pam Powers
For Harlequin Reader Service

## Complete the survey below and return it today to receive up to 4 FREE BOOKS and FREE GIFTS guaranteed!

# FREE BOOKS GIVEAWAY
## Reader Survey

### 1
**Do you prefer stories with happy endings?**

○ YES    ○ NO

### 2
**Do you share your favorite books with friends?**

○ YES    ○ NO

### 3
**Do you often choose to read instead of watching TV?**

○ YES    ○ NO

---

**YES!** Please send me my Free Rewards, consisting of **2 Free Books from each series I select** and **Free Mystery Gifts**. I understand that I am under no obligation to buy anything, as explained on the back of this card.

❏ **Harlequin Desire®** (225/326 HDL GQZ6)
❏ **Harlequin Presents® Larger-Print** (176/376 HDL GQZ6)
❏ **Try Both** (225/326 & 176/376 HDL GQ2J)

| | |
|---|---|
| FIRST NAME | LAST NAME |

ADDRESS

| | |
|---|---|
| APT.# | CITY |

| | |
|---|---|
| STATE/PROV. | ZIP/POSTAL CODE |

EMAIL ❏  Please check this box if you would like to receive newsletters and promotional emails from Harlequin Enterprises ULC and its affiliates. You can unsubscribe anytime.

HD/HP-520-FBG21

on. Still, Zora couldn't help feeling bad for the hurt feelings her actions had caused.

After they'd had dinner and her mother's delicious, homemade birthday cake, Zora sat at the table with her and Dallas's chairs pulled close together and his arm draped around her chair. She leaned into him, enjoying the warmth and comfort of her new husband's embrace.

A part of her couldn't help wishing this was real. That she and Dallas truly were romantic soulmates destined to be together, as their mothers had always believed.

# Fourteen

Dallas shrugged off his jeans and pulled his T-shirt over his head. He folded both and set them on top of the hamper in Zora's bathroom. Then he went back to her bedroom, where she was sitting in bed with her planner. A variety of writing utensils littered the bedspread.

"Sorry," she muttered, moving the pens and highlighters. "Not used to sharing my bed." Then Zora looked up at him, standing there in his black boxer briefs. "I…are you…is *that* what you're sleeping in?"

"Is this a problem?" Dallas spiked his fingers through his hair. They'd come straight to her place after her birthday dinner at her parents. All he had was his luggage from Vegas. So he didn't have a clean pair of shorts to sleep in. "If so, I'll have to go back to my place and grab a few things."

"No, of course not. I just…it…you surprised me,

that's all." Zora tore her errant gaze away from his package, her cheeks crimson. "You're fine. After all, I've seen you in much less, haven't I?"

Dallas chuckled as he climbed beneath the covers. "You certainly have. And if we plan on having sex, as it's a key factor in procreation, I suspect you'll see me in a lot less again." He winked.

Zora rolled her eyes. "But not until after we—"

"Both have a clean bill of health," he chimed in. "I'm on it. I'll make an appointment before I leave for Chicago in a few days."

"You're going to Chicago?" She frowned. "When?"

"I'll be gone most of next week. I'll text you the dates and add you to my business calendar. What about you? Don't you have some work travel planned?"

"Yes." She opened her planner and rattled off the dates for her scheduled trips to Atlanta and New York and an extended, two-week trip to four different countries in the European Union.

"Hmm...looks like our baby-making activities might require some coordination. Unless you'd like to come with me to Chicago," he suggested hopefully.

They tried their best to travel together at least once a year, when they weren't in relationships with other people. But even those trips had become more like working vacations. Both of them were attached to their phones and laptops, still responding to calls and emails. Still thinking about their respective businesses.

And though it was a business trip he was inviting her to join him on, he'd make sure that they found time to spend alone simply enjoying each other's company and planning for their future together.

"I can't just pick up and go to Chicago with you

next week, Dal," Zora said. "I have a ton of prep to do leading up to my sales trips. Besides, I would only be a distraction to you."

"You're not a *distraction*, Zora. You're my wife." It still felt foreign to say those words to his best friend.

Zora looked at him peculiarly when he said them, so it was evidently still strange for her to hear, too.

"I realize that, Dal. But this marriage doesn't negate the obligations I have to our company or that you have to yours." Zora softened her tone and expression as she delivered the very direct words.

"Right. Of course."

He tried not to sound disappointed that his wife had made it clear, in no uncertain terms, that their relationship ranked several rungs below her career. In fact, her father had to insist that she take off the rest of the week as a sort of a staycation honeymoon. Even then, Zora hadn't acquiesced until Duke had threatened, only half-jokingly, to have security remove her from the premises if she came to work the next day.

"About tonight at your parents'. Are you okay?" Dallas asked. She hadn't said much about their visit since they'd returned to her house. "I know things with Cole were a little tense tonight."

"I know, but it's fine." Zora shrugged.

But Dallas knew better. He could tell by the subtle slump of her slim shoulders and the hint of sadness in her dark brown eyes. She was genuinely hurt that her brothers were being assholes because their little sister— who was a fully grown adult, capable of making her own decisions, and of running the company, if given the chance—had gotten married without their blessing.

"Blake's and Max's feelings are hurt because their

little sister eloped. But with Cole…it feels like something deeper," he noted.

Zora frowned. "I know. I'll talk to him. *Eventually.*" She dropped the pens and highlighters into a pouch and zipped it, then put it and the planner on her nightstand. She turned out the lamp, shrouding her side of the room in darkness.

"I wouldn't have handled tonight well if you hadn't been there. Thank you for being my rock and the voice of reason. As always. And thank you for being patient with my brothers."

She leaned over to kiss his cheek, surprising him. He turned toward her suddenly, his lips crashing into hers. Zora pulled back, and studied him for a moment, neither of them speaking. Then she pressed a palm to his chest, leaned in and kissed him again.

She brushed her soft, sweet lips against his with a light, feathery touch that made him wonder for a moment if the kiss was real or if he'd only dreamed it.

Zora leaned into him, and he allowed her to dictate the intensity of their kiss. But when she parted her lips on a gasp, he couldn't resist sliding his tongue between her soft lips and tasting the mouth he'd been craving.

Dallas cradled her cheek, tilting her head to give him better access to her mouth. Then he pulled her closer so he could feel her lush curves crushed against his chest through the thin tank top she'd worn to bed with another little pair of sleep shorts.

Her nipples beaded, pressing against him through the fabric. She murmured in response, and he kissed her harder, swallowing the erotic sound that made his cock swell. Needing to hear it again and again.

Zora climbed onto him, straddling his lap. Her sex

pressed to his hardening length, making him groan with a growing desire for her.

Dallas gripped her bottom, pulling her closer as she kissed him, gliding her wet heat along his shaft through the barrier of their underwear. Making him crazy with need for her.

So many times he'd dreamed of kissing Zora. Of taking her to bed. Something he hadn't been proud of. Because crossing the line would jeopardize their friendship. Take them to a place they had agreed never to go. But he'd *wanted* to go there. And no matter how many times he'd chastised himself for thinking of Zora this way, his mind and body had other ideas.

Zora grazed his nipple with her thumb. An incidental touch that sent intense pleasure to his cock. He glided his fingertips up the soft skin of her back beneath the shirt, needing to have his bare skin on hers.

She broke away from the kiss, and his heart thudded in his chest, fearing that she was pulling away. But she kept her gaze on his as she tugged the shirt over her head and tossed it onto the floor, exposing her full breasts with their pebbled brown tips.

"Fuck, Zora." He whispered the words caught at the back of his throat. Dallas pressed a kiss to the base of her throat and another to her chest as he inhaled her sweet scent. He took one of the heavy globes in his hand, relishing its weight and size. She stroked his cheek, an intense hunger in her eyes as she arched her back. Her message clear.

Dallas's eyes drifted closed as he lowered his head, covering the offered morsel with his mouth. He savored her sensual murmurs and the way she dug her fingers into his hair as he teased her with little licks.

He rolled her onto her back and licked and sucked the hardened tip before moving to the other and doing the same. Then he kissed a trail down her soft belly and cupped her sex through the silky black panties shielding her wet heat.

Zora arched her back and groaned, tangling her fingers in his hair.

Dallas wanted to make love to her. More than anything. But Zora had just reminded him that they'd agreed to wait. He'd given her his word, and he'd honor their agreement, even if it meant he'd suffer from a killer case of blue balls for the rest of the night.

Dallas groaned, pausing for a moment to draw up the strength to tell her that they couldn't. Not tonight.

"Zora, I…" His eyes met hers.

"Oh God." She scrambled from beneath him, retrieved her shirt from the floor and put it back on. "I shouldn't have kissed you and I definitely shouldn't have…" She pressed a hand to her belly. "This one was definitely on me. I'm sorry."

"Don't be," he said gruffly, rolling onto his back on his designated side of the bed. "I wanted this, too." Dallas sighed. "But on the upside… When the time comes, lack of chemistry definitely won't be an issue."

A genuine smile spread across Zora's face and she dissolved into a fit of laughter. He couldn't help chuckling, too. It alleviated some of the tension in the room, like a pressure release valve had been opened.

Everything else between them felt so foreign right now. Sharing a laugh together was comforting and familiar.

Zora crawled back beneath the covers, clinging to

the edge of her side of the bed. As if there was a chasm between them.

Dallas turned off the light on his nightstand and folded his arm beneath his head as he stared at the ceiling. "'Night, Zo."

"Good night, Dallas."

The disappointment was as evident in her voice as it had been in his. But after two years of musing about what it would be like to make love to Zora, he could certainly wait another week.

They would be together soon enough.

# Fifteen

Zora parked in her designated spot in the King's Finest parking lot beside her brother Blake's luxury pickup truck. She sucked in a deep breath, grabbed her purse and the leather padfolio that held her iPad and bore her initials: ZAA. Only they weren't her initials anymore. Not according to the marriage license sitting on the desk in her home office.

She couldn't bring herself to display the document, but she couldn't bear to file it away, either. She'd looked at it every time she went into the office, as if she needed it there to remind her that she and Dallas were really married. If that hadn't convinced her, the fact that Dallas had spent every night in her bed since they'd returned home had made it quite apparent.

She'd arrived at the office an hour later than usual because she'd driven her husband to the airport for his weeklong trip to Chicago. And after a week of literally sleeping together and nothing more, she'd been nearly ready to combust when he'd leaned in and kissed her before he hopped out of the car.

Zora glanced up at the window of her office and blew out a slow breath. Her family had been uncharacteristically quiet all week. No calls from her parents or grandfather. No text messages from her brothers. Even Quinn and Savannah had given her and Dallas their space. But she had the feeling that the Abbott radio silence was a temporary moratorium while she and Dallas were on their stay-at-home honeymoon. Now that it was over, all bets were off.

Zora stepped out of her black-on-black Mercedes E 450 coupe with dark tinted windows.

*No matter how nervous you feel inside, walk with confidence. Shoulders back. Head held high.*

Zora could still hear her grandmother's sweet voice reciting those words to her when she was a slouching tween. It was still good advice.

She wouldn't go slinking into the office with her tail between her legs as if she was embarrassed by her hasty wedding. Instead, she would own it.

Zora pushed her Peyton Coco and Breezy shades up the bridge of her nose, tipped her chin and pulled her shoulders back as she strode toward the building in her cabernet-colored power suit, a bold cheetah-print blouse and cheetah-print booties.

The security guards at the gate congratulated her on her marriage, confirming what Zora already suspected. Everyone in town and at the distillery likely knew about her and Dallas's Vegas wedding.

Zora graciously accepted the congratulations of employees she encountered between the front door and her office. She patiently stopped to chat with each person briefly as they oohed and ahhed over the gorgeous pink sapphire engagement ring and diamond wedding band.

She spent a little more time chatting with her assistant, Emily, who'd been holding down the fort in her absence. The younger woman bounced on her heels excitedly when Zora approached and wrapped her in a big hug. Emily was genuinely excited for her, and the woman's enthusiasm was contagious.

"Your rings are gorgeous, and Dallas is such a sweetheart. Plus, you've been friends forever, so you already know everything about each other," Emily fawned. "You two are so lucky."

"I guess we are," Zora said, an involuntary smile tightening her cheeks. "Thanks."

"By the way, your father wants you to meet with him in the conference room at eleven. So we have some time to go over a few things first, if you'd like," Emily said excitedly.

"That'd be great, Em. Give me fifteen minutes?"

"Of course. And killer outfit… *Mrs*. Hamilton."

"Thank you, but Zora is fine, like always." Zora forced a smile and secured the topknot she'd pulled her curls up into, suddenly more conscious of the weight of the new hardware on her slim fingers.

"Zora, it is." Em could barely contain her grin. She sifted her fingers through her mermaid strands—dyed vibrant hues of purple, turquoise and blue. "Iced coffee?"

"Please," Zora said.

She'd gotten very little sleep during the past week. But for the opposite reason newlyweds were usually sleepless after their honeymoon. She and Dallas still hadn't had sex. Instead, she'd lain awake tossing and turning, her body thrumming with desire, knowing that her best friend—with his toned abs, hard chest and impressive package—lay just a couple of feet away from her wearing *very* little.

To add insult to injury, the last two nights she'd awakened cradled in his arms, the front of his hard body pressed to the back of hers. The first morning it happened, she'd freaked out a little. The second morning, she'd been slightly startled but had lain there until he awoke, enjoying the comfort, scent and warmth of him. Reveling in the affection he'd shown her, even unconsciously in his sleep.

Zora unlocked her office. "Emily, did my dad say what the meeting was about?"

"No. I tried to find out so you'd be prepared, but he was pretty tight-lipped about it," Emily said apologetically.

"Thanks for trying." Zora went inside her office and took a seat behind the desk.

The last two impromptu meetings she'd been called to were when her brother Parker had announced that he believed that he should be named the next CEO of King's Finest, rather than her oldest brother, Blake, whom they'd all assumed would take up their father's mantle whenever he decided to retire. And then when her father and grandfather had announced that they would indeed decide on the successor to the King's Finest throne based on merit—rather than birth order.

It was the first time she'd ever given thought to the possibility of heading up the company.

Even as a little girl, Zora had insisted that her parents

treat her equally to her brothers when it came to both privileges and chores. Her mother had been miffed. Her father had been impressed. And eventually, they'd both come to respect her request. So when the opportunity to lead the company was up for grabs, she'd insisted on being a candidate for CEO just like her brothers.

But since her grandfather's stroke—which occurred at that very meeting—there hadn't been much discussion among them about the succession plan. All their attention had gone to caring for her grandfather. Next, there was the revelation that Max and Quinn—who was heading up a new brandy initiative their company was rolling out—were indeed an item. Soon after that, Remi had been born.

The barrage of events had taken everyone's focus off the race to be the new CEO. Yet Zora doubted that any of them had taken their eyes off the prize.

She certainly hadn't.

So perhaps her father had called this morning's meeting because he'd made his decision. If so, she doubted that the timing was a coincidence. It could only mean that her hasty, surprise marriage had knocked her out of contention.

Zora did her best to shake off the negative energy.

*Don't be a self-defeatist. Until Dad says otherwise, you're still a contender for this thing.*

Suddenly, her phone alerted her to a text message.

*Dallas.*

He let her know that he'd boarded his plane and they'd be taking off soon. And he ended the text with a sentence that made her chest flutter.

Miss you already, Zo.

An involuntary smile lifted the corners of Zora's mouth, and without thought she pressed the phone to her chest. She missed him already, too.

Zora had enjoyed the time they'd spent together during the past week. She'd enjoyed chatting with her friend over coffee and working with him in the kitchen as they made breakfast and talked about their respective businesses.

The thing she'd avoided talking about was their plan to become co-parents. And admittedly, she'd taken her time scheduling the doctor's appointment she'd insisted on. Because while she was committed to the plan, she needed to be sure Dallas was, too.

She'd been pragmatic about sleeping with her best friend because she'd always been careful about her sex life. But she also wanted to give Dallas time to think about the commitment he was making with a clear mind. Without the mental haze and irrational thinking sex often precipitated.

So while Dallas was set and ready to go, her doctor's appointments were planned for the week while he was away. Then, if he returned and still wanted to move forward, she'd be ready. But until then, she was afraid to put too much of her heart into the idea of becoming a mother with Dallas. Because if the whole thing fell apart, she'd be heartbroken.

Zora sat behind her desk and reviewed Dallas's text message again. Then she typed her own reply.

Miss you, too. Call me when you land.

She resisted the urge to add XOXO. She'd often ended text messages that way in the past. But they were just friends then. Now they were something more. So signing the text message with hugs and kisses felt... different.

"Ready to go over my notes from last week?" Emily came bouncing into her office with her tablet, notepad and an iced coffee for Zora.

Zora dropped her phone, as if she'd been caught looking at an X-rated website on her work computer. She stood quickly, accepting the lifeline of caffeine.

Emily grinned at her, nodding toward her abandoned phone. "Got a text from hubby, huh?" She laughed in response to Zora's look of surprise, then answered the question she had yet to ask. "You're blushing and it's adorable. Y'all are so cute together."

Zora thanked the woman and flashed an awkward smile. "Now, about last week...what did I miss?"

Zora put on her game face and focused on what her assistant was saying. She shifted her brain from thoughts of buff best friends, bouncing babies and blown opportunities. Instead, she turned her attention to the thing she could control—her role in increasing the company's sales.

For now, everything else would have to wait.

"Zora, sweetheart, how are you?" Duke Abbott asked when she floated into the conference room about five minutes before their scheduled meeting.

But her father wasn't alone. All her brothers were there—including Cole, who rarely set foot in the distillery.

"Cole, what are you doing here?" Zora hadn't intended to ignore her father's greeting, but the fact that her brother was sitting in the chair typically occupied by her grandfather couldn't bode well. She glanced around the room. "And what's going on? If you guys say this is some kind of intervention, I swear to God—"

"Relax, Zo," Cole said.

"Zora, sweetheart, calm down," her father said simultaneously, rising to his feet.

Which, of course, only made her angry and more wary. In her experience, there was no better way to piss a woman off than to tell her to *relax*.

Zora set her padfolio on the table at her usual seat beside Max, but she refused to sit down. Instead, she folded her arms and stared around the table at each of them.

"Not until you all tell me what this is about."

"Zora, I'm sorry if you feel like you're being ambushed. That wasn't our intention." Parker cleared his throat. "We'd like to talk to you about a few things, that's all. No reason for alarm. Please, have a seat."

There was a soft, pleading look in her brother's eyes that threw Zora off her game. So now Parker was the quiet, compassionate voice of reason?

Zora pulled out her chair and took a seat, sliding away from Max, who had yet to speak.

*Traitor.*

"I have a lot to do today." She turned to her father. "So if someone could please tell me what this is all about?"

"Your brothers are concerned that in your haste to marry Dallas, you might've overlooked a few things. We just want to ensure that your interests and the family's are protected." Her father's expression was kind and his voice was as soothing as a warm bath.

"Why would you be concerned about me or the family's interests?" She glanced around the table. Cole and Max looked the most uncomfortable. Neither of them was giving her direct eye contact. So she went on the offensive, calling them both out. "Cole. Max. You two evidently orchestrated this whole thing. So don't act shy and delicate now. Let's hear it. Whatever you brought me here to say, *say it*."

"Look, brat, you know we all adore you," Max said. "But we can't stand by and not say anything when you've made an impetuous decision that could negatively impact you—"

"And us," Parker chimed in, his expression almost apologetic. "More importantly, Grandad's legacy." He gestured to the space around them.

"First, don't call me brat. I'm thirty-two fucking years old." She pointed a finger at Max. "Second, yes, our decision to get married was unexpected, but it was hardly a surprise to any of the *women* in our family. Third, how on earth would my decision to get married impact any of you? You didn't see me throwing a fit when any of you hooked up with your significant others." She glanced around the table accusingly.

"You're right," Max said, his open palms held up. "You're a smart, capable woman, and you've certainly outgrown the nickname, if you ever deserved it."

Zora relaxed a little and nodded at her brother. "Thank you."

"But c'mon, Zo, if any of us had gone to Vegas for the weekend and come back married, you'd be all over us about it," Cole interjected.

*Fair.*

"If it were some stranger you'd met at a blackjack table, maybe," Zora said. "Dallas isn't some stranger.

He's an honorary member of this family. We've all known him since he and I were in kindergarten."

"Which is why we don't understand your sudden rush to get married." Blake's voice was calm and reasonable. "Especially since you've both always claimed that the relationship was platonic."

"It was." *It* is. *Kind of.*

"Then why the sudden marriage?" Max asked, his voice tentative.

"You told Savannah that you want to have kids. Is that because you're already pregnant?" Cole asked, his eyes finally meeting hers dead-on.

"No!" Zora responded immediately. She balled her hands into fists and counted to ten in her head. "But if I was pregnant, that would be *my* business." She glanced around the room at her brothers, all of whom looked varying degrees of uncomfortable. She pushed to her feet, her hands pressed to the table. "What? You don't believe me? Would you like me to pee on a stick for you, Cole?"

"That won't be necessary." Duke raised a hand, seemingly unnerved by the whole conversation.

*Y'all started this.*

Her grandmother had always said, "Don't start nothing, won't be nothing." It had been her motto in school when dealing with mean girls and bullies.

She'd tried to be nice to everyone and never started conflicts. But if someone else chose to initiate one, putting an end to the bullshit was her great gift.

"Look, I'm sorry." Cole sighed. "I was out of line. I'm just saying…this doesn't feel like you, Zora. Not at all. Hell, I half expected you to commission a tiara, a horse-drawn carriage and a release of doves for your wedding. So I don't get why you'd get married all of a sudden in Vegas without telling any of your family. Not even me." He seemed really hurt by that last bit.

Was that what this was really all about? Cole was upset because she hadn't confided in him about her "plan" to get married?

Zora heaved a quiet sigh and recalled how Dallas had pleaded with her to be patient with her family. To understand why they'd be so hurt by being left out of their wedding.

"Like I said before, we didn't go there intending to get married. This all just sort of…happened. But now that it has, it feels right and we're both happy. I wish you could be as happy for us as I was for each of you when you connected with your current partners." She shifted her gaze from Blake to Parker and then to Max. All of whom had the decency to at least look slightly ashamed of themselves.

Parker cleared his throat and spoke up. "We appreciate your support, Zora. And we… I *am* happy for you," he said after surveying his brothers' grim faces. "But since your wedding was spontaneous, I'm assuming you two didn't sign the prenuptial agreement we all agreed to use five years ago. The one designed to ensure King's Finest will always stay in our family instead of going to someone else."

*Shit. Should have known that would come up.*

If she'd married some random stranger, she'd be worried. But this was Dallas they were talking about. She trusted her friend. With her life, if need be.

"You're right." She slid into her seat. "We all agreed to use prenuptial agreements to protect KFD. But you're worried that we can't trust Dallas? Why would he try to take a portion of our company? He has his own and it's doing well."

"Dallas Hamilton is an upstanding, hardworking, successful young man, and I know he cares deeply for you, Zora," her father countered. "It isn't that we don't trust him, per se."

"Then what is it?" She glanced around the room, her heart thumping and her eyes burning with tears of anger that she blinked away.

"It's just better to be safe than sorry, Zo." Max clapped a hand over hers and squeezed it gently. "None of us are attributing bad motives to Dallas. But people and circumstances can change. It's something we can't predict. So it's better to cover all the bases."

"And since Dallas is doing so well, as you said, he shouldn't mind signing a postnuptial agreement to clearly delineate your assets," Parker noted. "In fact, it seems like it would be to his advantage, too."

"And the terms of the agreement are very generous," Blake reminded her. "So Dallas—or any of our former spouses," he added when Zora narrowed her gaze at him, "would still come out ahead. Not that we anticipate your marriage ending, Zora. Or any of ours, for that matter."

Zora stared at Blake, her heart beating rapidly. Maybe her brother really didn't believe that her marriage to Dallas would end any time soon. But given that she knew the truth about the temporary nature of their relationship, asking Dallas to enter into an agreement that would pay him a generous settlement on the dissolution of their marriage seemed unwise.

She pulled her hand from Max's and stood again. "No," she said quietly. "I appreciate your concern, but

I'm not asking Dallas to sign a postnuptial. So if there isn't anything else, I have a lot of catching up to do."

Zora grabbed her padfolio from the table and left the room. She'd nearly reached her office when Cole caught up with her.

He stepped around in front of her and lowered his voice so no one else could hear him. "Is this about that Icelandic deal Dallas is trying to do?"

"What are you talking about?" Her eyes widened.

"Tish was telling us about it before you all arrived at Mom and Dad's last week. I looked up that guy Dallas is trying to collaborate with. Did you two enter a sham marriage because Dallas thinks he'll have a better chance of entering into a deal with the man if he's married rather than a bachelor?"

"That's ridiculous." Zora wrapped her arms around the padfolio and held it to her chest, hoping it dampened the sound of her raging heartbeat. She stood taller and tipped her chin, looking her brother squarely in the eye. "Seriously, Cole. Do you really think I would've given up my horse-drawn carriage and flight of doves for that?"

She started to walk away again, but her brother braced a hand on her arm and lowered his voice more.

"You're a good person and a loyal friend, Zora. And I know how much you care for Dallas. So, yes, I believe you'd make that kind of sacrifice for him. Just like you did when you helped finance his business."

"How'd you know about that?" Zora snatched her arm away from Cole's and frowned, her words a harsh whisper.

"I wasn't sure," Cole admitted. "But I've always suspected."

"Dallas never asked me for a penny. In fact, it took me months to convince him to accept my *investment* in his business." She stressed the word. "And as you can see, my gamble paid off. He paid every cent back with interest years ago. But please don't—"

"I won't say anything to anyone else about this," Cole assured her. "But you're my kid sister. I won't let anyone take advantage of your generous nature."

"Cole, I know you love me and that you're just trying to look out for me here but listen to me carefully. If you think my marriage is the result of some arrangement where Dallas is taking advantage of our friendship, you honestly couldn't be more wrong about him. Now please, have a little faith in me. After all, I've always had faith in you."

Before her brother could respond, Zora's phone vibrated in her pocket. She pulled it out, looked at the caller ID and smiled.

*Dallas.*

"That would be my husband calling to let me know he's landed safely. I assume we're done here?"

Cole sighed and nodded. "See you later, Zo."

Zora watched her brother head back toward the conference room. Then she answered the call.

She couldn't ever remember being happier to hear Dallas's voice.

# Sixteen

The event Dallas had been scheduled to attend on Sunday morning—the last of his seven-day trip to Chicago—had been canceled. So he booked an earlier flight home.

Normally, Dallas would've used his windfall of free time to enjoy the city, sketch out design ideas, or read a good book. But from the moment he'd learned of the cancellation, he'd had just one thought: Zora.

So he'd paid the obscene fees to change his flight and taken a ride share back to his place to drop off his luggage, because he wanted to surprise his wife. Dallas grabbed some fresh clothes and a few other essential items. Just enough to get him through the next few days back at Zora's place. Then he slipped the letter from his doctor's office into the inside pocket of his matte black leather jacket with the word *Triumph* curved across the back in a barely visible, tonal print.

Dallas put the clothing in the saddlebags of his motorcycle—a Triumph Thruxton RS he'd treated himself to a year ago—and slipped on his black, matte Icon AirFlite helmet. Then he threw his right leg over the bike, settling onto the seat and placing his booted feet flat on the ground before turning the key in the ignition. After a few minutes warming up, he eased off the clutch, rolling the bike out of his driveway, before finally giving it some throttle once he hit the road.

It was early afternoon on a beautiful fall day. The sun shone through the trees, illuminating the vivid red, bright gold and glowing orange leaves still clinging to the branches. He loved riding at this time of year, the wind swirling around him as he reveled in the freedom of the road. But today he had a single focus: he had every intention of finally making love to his beautiful wife.

There was a churning in the pit of Dallas's stomach. He wasn't nervous about finally being with Zora. He'd been distracted all week by images of her naked beneath him in the bed they shared. The thing that unsettled him was the realization that this would change things between them forever.

His desire for Zora would come out of the shadows and be lain undeniably bare. Where neither of them could pretend it wasn't there. They'd agreed to go back to being friends at the end of a year. But what were the chances the genie would quietly return to the bottle?

The second thing that had been weighing on his mind was that he and Zora were about to embark on this journey toward becoming parents.

The enormity of what they were undertaking came into perspective the moment he'd lain eyes on Remi and

stroked her soft skin. She looked so small and defense-
less. And as he looked onto the baby girl's sleeping face,
he couldn't help wondering what his and Zora's child
would look like.

Would the child have its mother's bright smile and
inquisitive eyes? His strong chin? Would her skin re-
semble her mother's gorgeous terra cotta brown skin or
fall somewhere on the spectrum between Zora's rich,
deep skin tone and his? Would she have her mother's
fiery personality and infectious laugh or his laid-back
demeanor and off sense of humor?

Dallas gave the bike more throttle as he hurtled toward Duke and Iris's house, where Zora would be along
with the rest of her siblings and their mates. He'd like
nothing more than to kidnap her, put her on the back of
his bike and head back to her place, where he'd spend
the rest of the day ravishing the body he'd been dreaming about in great detail.

He finally pulled onto the road that led past the barn
and toward Zora's parents' place at the end of the street.
Dallas parked the bike in his new in-laws' driveway,
removed his helmet and made his way to the open side
door.

As always, Iris Abbott's kitchen smelled heavenly.
The scents of fresh-baked bread, savory meat, fra-
grant vegetables and enticing desserts teased his nostrils. But he wouldn't allow himself to be distracted by
Iris's amazing food. Not now.

Making his way quietly up the few steps, he entered
the kitchen where Zora, her mother, Quinn, Kayleigh
and Savannah were gathered. Kayleigh and Quinn were
busy making a salad. Iris was stirring a pot on the stove.
Savannah sat on a bar stool, a blanket draped over her

as she presumably fed baby Remi. Zora stood in front of her, a dish towel in her hand as the two women chatted.

Zora looked both sexy and adorable, her curly hair gathered in a messy bun. She wore a burgundy suede skirt that grazed her midthigh, a black turtleneck and black thigh-high boots that had him salivating.

Sitting through a meal next to Zora in that outfit, when what he really wanted to do was get her home and out of it, would be pure torture.

Dallas crept inside, walking as lightly as possible in the heavy black leather boots. He waved at Iris, but held a finger up to his mouth, imploring her to play along as he sneaked up on his unsuspecting wife. Iris grinned, as did Quinn and Kayleigh when they caught a glimpse of him. Savannah gave him the slightest head nod, so as not to tip off Zora.

In one smooth move, Dallas slipped his arms around Zora's waist and dropped a tender kiss on her neck.

Startled, she jumped but didn't scream. She turned around in his arms, her brown eyes gazing up at his. Her expression quickly shifted from surprise to genuine happiness at seeing him. Something about it made his heart dance.

"Dallas, what are you doing here? Your flight isn't scheduled to land until later this evening."

"I know." He tightened his grip on her waist, pulling her closer, his eyes not leaving hers. "I couldn't wait to see you, babe."

Dallas stared at his wife, unsure of how she would react to such a public display of affection. But she'd told him about how Cole doubted whether their marriage was genuine. What better way to prove those doubts wrong?

For a few moments, it felt as if time had slowed. The entire kitchen, which had been filled with chatter and laughter when he'd arrived, was suddenly silent. But Zora lifted onto her toes, looped her arms around his neck and dragged his mouth down to hers as she pressed a soft kiss to his lips. They were greeted by a chorus of awws.

Zora pulled back, glancing up at him. "Missed you, too. I'm glad you came home early."

"Speaking of home," Iris said, not so subtly. "Why don't you and Dallas head there? Your husband must be exhausted after his long week in Chicago without his boo."

Quinn, Kayleigh and Savannah all giggled.

"I can't skip out on dinner." Zora glanced over at her mother. "We haven't even eaten yet."

"Not a problem. I'll have your meals packed and ready to go in a few minutes. That'll give Dallas just enough time to go in and say hello to the boys."

Zora opened her mouth to object, but Quinn put a hand on her shoulder.

"Really, Zora, we understand," Quinn assured her. "Take your man and your meal and go home. There'll be plenty more Sunday meals with the family."

"Fine. We know when we're not wanted," Zora said.

"I'd love to have you all stay and have dinner with us, but I remember what it was like to be a newlywed," Iris said. "And with your busy schedules, you should make the most of every moment you two have to spend together."

"I agree." Dallas took Zora's hand and strode into the family room, where her father, grandfather, brothers and nephew were watching a football game.

Dallas greeted the men, shaking her father's and grandfather's hands. Parker, Max and Blake's greetings seemed warm and genuine, closer to what he was accustomed to from each of them. Cole nodded his greeting, but anger still brewed behind his dark eyes.

"We're not staying for dinner," Zora said sheepishly. "Dallas just landed, and he's had a really long week. Mom insists that I take him home to get some rest. She's packing our meals to go."

"Too tired to eat, huh?" Joseph Abbott snickered. "I wasn't always this old, you know."

"Leave the kids alone, Dad." Duke chuckled. He turned his attention back to them. "We understand. I don't think the world will end if Zora and Dallas miss a meal or two with us."

"Thanks for understanding," Dallas said to the two men.

"I was looking out the window at your motorcycle, Dallas," Grandpa Joseph said. "Mighty fancy bike you've got there. I remember when those café racers were popular. You restore that thing yourself?"

"No, sir," he admitted. "And this isn't a restoration. It's a brand-new bike made with the retro styling but all the modern bells and whistles."

"I like it." Zora's grandfather nodded approvingly. "And you certainly look the part, son." Grandpa Joe indicated his motorcycle jacket and boots. "You plan on whisking my granddaughter away on that thing?"

"Not today, Gramps," Zora said quickly. She squeezed Dallas's hand. "But maybe I'll let him take me for a ride, *eventually*."

Dallas grinned. It was the first time Zora had ever shown any interest in riding on the bike.

"Seems dangerous," Parker offered. "You have life insurance and a living will, right?"

"Wow, Park. Way to kill the mood." Max chuckled.

"What?" Parker shrugged. "Have you seen the accident statistics for those things?"

Dallas and Zora spent some time showing Davis his bike through the window and answering the little boy's barrage of questions until Zora's mother appeared.

She handed them a cloth bag stacked with glass storage containers. "Got your food all packed."

Dallas released Zora's hand and accepted the bag. He leaned down and kissed his mother-in-law on the cheek. "Thank you, Iris."

"Of course." She grinned. "And no pressure, hon, but I wouldn't be opposed to you calling me Mom."

Iris's words simultaneously warmed his chest and broke his heart. His marriage to Zora would end in a year. He'd lose the privilege of calling Iris Mom nearly as quickly as he'd gained it.

"Thanks, Mom." Dallas smiled. Then he took Zora's hand and they said their goodbyes.

# Seventeen

Zora pulled her Mercedes into her pristine, attached, two-car garage, and Dallas parked his bike in the empty space beside it. Then she hit the button to lower the garage door and stepped out of the car.

She glanced over at Dallas, and a shiver ran down her spine. The man looked incredibly sexy in a black motorcycle jacket, a matte black helmet that made him look mysterious and maybe even a little dangerous, and a pair of heavy motorcycle boots. The thought of him commanding all that power thrumming between his strong thighs…well, it was enough to make a girl go weak at the knees.

*That* was the reason she had never agreed to hop onto the back and ride with him when he offered. That and the fact that she was an unabashed control freak. It was hard enough to be the passenger in a plane or car. But sitting on the back of a motorcycle careening down a mountain road and taking hairpin curves with absolutely no say or control? It was an adventure she wasn't quite ready for.

Dallas engaged the kickstand and climbed off his bike, removing the helmet and hanging it on the back of the motorcycle. He dragged his fingers through his hair and grinned.

"You're a sight for sore eyes." His gaze roamed the length of her body, and her skin pricked with heat beneath his hungry gaze.

Zora sank her teeth into her lower lip and tried not to think about how delicious her husband looked.

"You can cut the act. We're alone now."

Yep, she was pathetically fishing for a compliment. Dallas Hamilton definitely had her off her game.

"It's no act, Zora." He stopped a few feet shy of her. "I told you, if we do this…it has to be real for however long we're together. I meant what I said." His whiskey-brown eyes had darkened and were hooded as he gazed down at her with a heated stare.

Her nipples beaded, and she could feel the dampness between her thighs. Zora swallowed hard, one hand going inadvertently to her neck. As if she needed to protect it.

"You called me *babe* earlier." She shifted her gaze from his increasingly intense one. "You've never called me that before."

"To be fair, we've never been married before. So there are a lot of things we haven't done." His lips curved in a cocky, half-grin. "Problem?"

"No," she whispered, shaking her head.

Dallas moved closer, so less than a foot separated

them now. Yet he still hadn't touched her. And she couldn't help being disappointed by his restraint. But the promise he'd made when they first made their agreement in Vegas replayed in her head.

*Nothing happens unless you want it to.*

She wanted it to. God, did she want it. She thought of him often, her fingers gliding over the damp space between her thighs as she lay in the bed that felt so much emptier without him.

A heavy silence lingered between them, filled only with the sound of her breathing, growing shallower and more rapid by the moment.

"Got you a little something." Dallas retrieved an unopened envelope from the inside of his leather jacket and handed it to her, his eyes never leaving hers.

Zora glanced down at the envelope branded with the name of a local medical practice.

*His all clear.*

She had already texted him the results of the battery of tests she'd taken. So there were no more excuses. No reason why she couldn't do the thing she'd wanted to do for the past two weeks. The thing she fantasized about a time or two long before they'd awakened married in Vegas.

"I guess we're all good, then." She handed it back.

"You don't want to open it?" he asked.

"I trust you, Dallas." Zora took a step backward, finding it more difficult to breathe with Dallas so close. The smell of his enticing cologne mingled with the scent of the crisp, autumn air was slightly intoxicating.

He stepped forward and she retreated again, her bottom pressed against the door of the Mercedes. "I appre-

ciate the vote of confidence. But a deal is a deal, right?"
He handed the envelope back to her.

Zora fumbled with it, ripping it open. She could
barely focus her vision enough to make sense of the
jumble of black letters on the pages. "Everything looks
good." She handed the envelope back to him.

Dallas returned the letter to his inside jacket pocket.
Zora's eyes were drawn to the way his Adam's apple
bobbed when he swallowed and the scruff on his chin.

She wanted to kiss the same path her eyes had just
taken along his skin. And she wanted to feel the slight
burn of that scruff as he trailed kisses down her belly,
as he had that first night in her bed when she'd lost control and kissed him.

Zora swallowed hard, her eyes meeting his again.
Her heart raced, and her hands were shaking. Dallas
was really and truly going to make her say the words.
Be the one to ask for it. She could see it in his dark eyes.
He wanted to hear her beg.

She honestly had no qualms about asking for what
she wanted in bed, demanding it, even. But he was her
best friend, and this all still felt so…strange. Still, she
wanted him. More importantly, she needed him.

Dallas Hamilton had been the perfect fuel for her
lust-filled fantasies. But she needed something a little
more…*solid*…right now.

Zora allowed her hands to trail below his leather belt
and traced the ridge beneath the zipper of his jeans. A
soft, almost tortured sigh escaped her friend's mouth,
his breath warm on her skin. A wicked little smile
curved her mouth. She was eager to elicit that same
reaction again.

This time, Zora opened her hand as wide as she

could and gripped his stiff length through the thick denim. Her fingers glided down the outline of his growing shaft, and she cupped him at its base. Dallas made a sound she wouldn't quite call a whimper, but it was pretty damn close.

"Fuck, Zora," he whispered, leaning into her hand, his eyes drifting closed momentarily. Dallas placed his hands against the car on either side of her.

It was exhilarating to be pinned between him and the car. Yet it was empowering to know she was capable of bringing her friend to his knees. Zora unzipped his black leather jacket the rest of the way. Then she eased her hands over his skin, beneath the fabric of his soft, brushed-cotton T-shirt. She flicked his taut nipples with her thumb and lifted onto her toes.

"Kiss me, Dallas," she whispered breathlessly. "Please."

He leaned down and covered her mouth with his own, his thumbs caressing her cheekbones. This kiss wasn't tentative, as their previous kisses had been. It was greedy and demanding. Intense and hungry. A side of himself Dallas rarely showed.

Zora gripped his back beneath the shirt, hoping her short nails wouldn't leave marks. She lost herself in the kiss, her body aching with need for him. Her keys had fallen out of her hand and onto the garage floor long ago.

She didn't care. All she cared about was getting naked and letting her husband make love to her.

Zora fumbled with Dallas's belt, finally unbuckling the stubborn item as they continued their kiss. She slipped her hand beneath the waistband of his boxers.

This time they both groaned with satisfaction as she fisted his heated skin.

"Fuck," he muttered as she glided her palm up and down his rock-hard shaft. "God, I wish this was anything but your fancy-ass Mercedes. I'd lift you onto the top of this thing, spread you open and have the only meal I care about right now."

She halted her movement, the vision sending a shudder down her spine, making her knees weak and her sex weep.

Zora swallowed roughly. She was just about to tell him that the dent in the hood would be totally worth it when he backed away.

"We'd better get this food into the house," he said, his chest heaving. "And I'm going to grab a shower. Then I plan to pick up *exactly* where we left off."

Zora nodded as Dallas opened the door, reached in and grabbed the bag of food her mother had packed, his perfect ass on display.

Yes, she was *definitely* going to enjoy this.

Dallas shrugged his clothes off onto the floor and stepped into the steaming-hot shower in the other master bedroom. He typically showered and shaved in this bathroom, since Zora had everything in hers neatly arranged. Every spot was filled with some kind of facial cleanser, foundation, eye shadow or mascara.

The fact that there wasn't enough room for him and his things in Zora's bathroom was a perfect metaphor for his concerns about their relationship. She was the only person in his life who hadn't needed him in one way or another.

Even now, she didn't really need his help. She had

the situation all planned out and she had the means to execute that plan on her own.

The neat little box he'd fit into in Zora's life was as her friend. Did a woman as self-reliant as Zora have room for him in her life?

After sudsing his entire body, Dallas stepped beneath the spray to rinse himself off. Then he pressed a hand against the cool tile, stuck his head beneath the spray of hot water to rinse the shampoo from his hair and sighed.

Suddenly, the glass shower door opened, ushering in a gust of cool air and releasing the steam.

"Zora." He could barely get the word out of his throat. His friend stepped into the shower. Every inch of her glorious brown skin was exposed, leaving him speechless.

Dallas looped one arm around her waist. He trailed the other over the curve of her ass as she leaned into him.

"Thought you might like some company." Her dark eyes glinted as she flashed an impish smile. "Then there was that thing about picking up where we left off." She shrugged. "I got a little impatient."

Dallas brushed his lips along her temple, then pressed a kiss there. He pressed another on the shell of her ear. "You are so incredibly beautiful, Zora," he whispered. "And I can't wait to make love to my wife."

He nibbled on her ear and she giggled.

"Your temporary wife?" she asked. "I think she's looking forward to this, too."

"I prefer to think of you as my wife, *full stop*." Dallas cupped her cheek, his eyes meeting hers. He needed her to see that he meant what he was saying. "Not my temporary wife. Not my future ex. Just my wife, who also happens to be my best friend."

"I like that," she whispered, leaning into him and wrapping her arms around his back, her short nails digging into his skin.

He kissed her, exploring the sweet taste of her mouth as he sucked her lower lip between his own. His hands explored her smooth skin and delicious curves, which he appreciated all the more for seeing them in their full glory.

Dallas trailed kisses down her neck, then took one of the heavy, brown globes in his hand, kissing and sucking the pebbled tip as Zora squirmed and moaned quietly, her back pressed against the tiled wall. He trailed his hand down her belly and over the small patch of thick, dark curls between her thighs. He moved his fingers back and forth over the bundle of nerves, kissing her mouth again to swallow her quiet whimpers. Then he plunged one finger, then another, inside her.

"God, Zora. You are so wet for me," he whispered in her ear. "But I think we can do better than this."

Dallas dropped to his knees on the hard tile floor, his hands on her hips. Zora stared at him wordlessly, her eyes wide, as he eased her bottom onto the edge of the black tiled bench and gently pressed her knees apart, widening the space between them. Then he dipped his head and tasted her there.

Zora released a breathless whimper and spiked her fingers into his hair. Her moans grew louder, more desperate, as he licked and sucked her sensitive flesh. The escalation of her encouraging commands and desperate little pleas made him as hard as steel. He added two fingers inside her as his tongue continued to work its magic.

She arched her back. Her feet flexed, lifting onto her toes. Her body tensed and her legs shook. The way she whimpered his name made him want to take her right there in the shower with her hands splayed against the wall and one foot propped on the tile bench.

But this would be their first time together, and he wanted to take his time with her. Show her just how good things between them could be, if only she gave them a chance.

Dallas stood and turned off the water. He drew Zora into his arms and kissed her. Slowly and tenderly, at first. But the fire and passion between them built. Her kiss became hungrier, and his was downright greedy. Because he honestly didn't think he could ever get enough of her.

He wrapped his arms around her waist, pulling her tighter against his painfully hard dick. Dallas ached with his desire to be buried balls-deep inside his ridiculously sexy wife. The woman he hadn't been able to stop thinking about for the past week.

Maybe their marriage was only temporary. But he was still a lucky bastard, getting to come home to this gorgeous woman each night and share a bed with her.

With the hot water turned off, the temperature around them cooled and Zora started shivering.

Dallas tore his mouth from Zora's plump, kiss-swollen lips just long enough to get them both toweled off and over to Zora's bed at the opposite end of the upstairs hall.

They climbed beneath the luxurious white duvet and soft Egyptian cotton sheet, their naked bodies still damp from the shower.

"May I?" Dallas indicated the band that held Zora's hair back in a messy bun. When she nodded, he took it off, releasing the loose ringlets that had been stretched by the tension. Dallas sifted the soft, silky curls through his fingers, as he'd imagined doing so many times before.

"You are so beautiful, Zora." Dallas grazed her cheek with his callused thumb as he stared down into those hypnotic brown eyes.

Dallas captured her full lips in an intense kiss. As the heat between them built to a fever pitch, he gripped his shaft, pressing it to her slick entrance and slowly penetrating. He reveled in every ounce of pleasure that rolled up his spine as he inched inside her until he was fully seated.

Dallas kissed her again, forcing himself to take it slowly as he moved inside her. Determined to savor every moment.

But as their kisses grew more intense, so did the power and speed with which he moved his hips.

"Oh God, Dallas. Yes. *Yes.* Just like that. Don't stop. *Please.*" Zora's fervent pleas escalated as their bodies, now damp with sweat, moved together. Each of them hurtling closer to the edge.

He repositioned her leg, lifting it over his hip and changing the angle of impact.

She responded immediately.

Panting and breathless, Zora cried out his name.

Her hair was wild, and beads of sweat trickled down her forehead and neck. But Zora was sexier than he'd ever seen her before.

Her sex pulsed, tightening its grip on his shaft. Dallas rode the waves of Zora's pleasure until he'd hurtled into a sea of bliss. One he hoped to revisit again and again.

His back arched and his muscles strained as he spilled every ounce of himself inside her. Finally, he tumbled onto his back, his chest heaving.

Zora propped one of the many pillows on her bed beneath her bottom, presumably to allow gravity to get his little swimmers where they needed to go.

They both lay there, breathing heavily as they stared at the ceiling in silence.

Finally, his breath slowed. "That was—"

"Weird...right?" she offered.

"Definitely not the word I was going for." Dallas chuckled, turning onto his side and sweeping loose curls away from her face. "I was gonna say fucking amazing."

"Sorry, I totally should've led with that, because yeah, it was *definitely* that." Zora gave him a quick kiss. "But also...weird, right? Because it's us. But then, maybe that's what made it so amazing, too."

"Always wondered what this would be like. The moment certainly didn't disappoint." He kissed her neck.

"You thought about this *before*? Like before we woke up married?" She pressed a hand to his chest, halting him from going in for another kiss.

"And you haven't?" He hiked an eyebrow.

"Not the point, Hamilton." Streaks of crimson kissed Zora's cheeks and dotted her chest.

"What is the point?" He nuzzled her neck with his nose and flicked one pebbled brown nipple with his thumb.

"Round two." She whispered the words roughly. "But after we fuel up in the kitchen."

Dallas surveyed her mischievous smile, his own grin deepening. He chuckled. "I definitely like the sound of that."

# Eighteen

Zora strolled into the kitchen, dressed for work in a casual navy pantsuit and a white blouse, unable to shake herself from her blissful haze. Dallas had already brewed a pot of coffee and the aroma of sizzling bacon made her mouth water.

She'd awakened that morning wrapped in Dallas's arms, as she had many nights before. But this time was different. They were both still naked after a night of making love and getting acquainted with each other's bodies. And when she'd tried to ease out of his grip and make her way to the bathroom to get ready for work, she'd inadvertently roused him from his sleep.

He'd blinked drowsily for a moment before he'd gained clarity. But then he'd greeted her with the most adorable smile.

Dallas always had a way of smiling at her when

they'd seen each other again for the first time in months that made her feel…special. As if she were the most important person in his world. But the look in his eyes that morning had practically made her melt into a puddle of goo, like some old-school cartoon character.

"Hello, beautiful," he'd murmured gruffly.

What was the proper morning greeting for your best friend who also happened to be your temporary spouse and future baby daddy?

*A fist bump? A kiss on the cheek? Maybe a peck on the lips?*

"Good morning, Dal. Sorry I woke you, but I need to get ready for work."

"Or you could ditch work today and stay in bed with me." He'd nuzzled her ear and gripped her waist with seemingly no intention of releasing his hold. "I promise to make it worth your while."

"I…umm…" She'd cleared her throat, unable to string together a coherent sentence. "Em and I are leaving in a couple of days, so—"

"Which is why you should stay in bed with me today." He'd nibbled on her ear and grazed her nipple with the roughened pad of his thumb.

"I took nearly a week off for our honeymoon. That was just two weeks ago," she'd objected half-heartedly.

"But we weren't having sex then, which is kind of the point of a honeymoon," Dallas had said as he trailed kisses down her neck.

"Is it, though?" Zora had tried her best to seem unaffected by his touch. "I thought it was to destress from the wedding by spending time alone together."

"And having sex." He'd kissed her chest, his sensual mouth pulling into a flirtatious smirk. "Lots of it."

When he'd nuzzled her neck and feathered kisses over her heated skin, that was all it took for her to settle right back into bed with him.

"Hey, babe." Dallas leaned down and kissed her neck, bringing her out of her erotic daze.

He was shirtless and wearing a pair of jeans commando, slung low on his hips. Zora's eyes went immediately to the light brown trail of hair on his stomach that disappeared below the waistband of his jeans. Suddenly, memories of the shower they'd taken together that morning—where he'd taken her again, up against the shower wall—flashed vividly in her brain.

She shut her eyes against the image and cleared her throat. "Hey. I see you made breakfast," she said.

Dallas chuckled, as if he could see the naughty images flashing in her head. "It was the least I could do after throwing you off schedule this morning. I know you like things just so. Have a seat."

He indicated one of the stools at the breakfast bar as he arranged four slices of bacon on each of their plates.

Zora was going to object. It was already later than she usually arrived at the office. But Dallas had gone to all the trouble of making this breakfast for them while she got dressed and put on her makeup. It seemed rude to turn it down. Besides, banging like a couple of horny teenagers apparently made you voraciously hungry.

It suddenly became quite clear why Blake, Parker and Max had started coming into the office later and leaving earlier than they had before they'd gotten into relationships.

"Thank you." She slid onto the stool and took a sip from the glass of orange juice he'd set in front of her. "This was sweet of you. But you didn't have to do this. I could've grabbed something on the way to the office."

"Then I wouldn't have had the pleasure of having a meal with my wife," he said, sliding scrambled eggs onto their plates.

"You like saying that word, don't you?" Zora set her glass down.

"What word? *Wife*?" Dallas glanced at her curiously, then smiled sheepishly when she confirmed as much with a nod. He shrugged. "I hadn't thought about it, but I guess maybe I do."

Dallas spread some of his mother's homemade strawberry preserves on a slice of toast.

Zora refrained from asking the question that burned on the tip of her tongue.

*Why?*

All this was designed as smoke and mirrors to conceal the less-than-romantic truth from their families— that they'd gotten high as two kites in a windstorm and gotten married in a Vegas chapel. That they'd stayed married because she wanted to have a child but wasn't willing to wait for a theoretical spouse to give her one.

But pretending as if this was truly a marriage *here*, when they were alone, felt like a dangerous game with the potential of consuming them, leaving one or both of them hurt. And despite the crazy circumstances in which they found themselves, the last thing she wanted to do was to hurt her friend.

Dallas Hamilton was a rugged man who loved the outdoors. He made the most gorgeous furniture with his beautiful, intricate brain and his talented hands. But he was also sensitive and sweet in a way that most men she knew weren't.

He protected that soft underbelly by being careful about whom he let in. It was the reason none of his past relationships had been serious. He was still fiercely protecting the heart of that little boy who'd been crushed when his father walked away.

She would do everything in her power to protect that kind, loving little boy, too. So it was up to her to keep them both on track. To remind them of the plan whenever they began to veer away from it.

"What's on your agenda for today?" Zora asked brightly. "Are you working out of the Hamilton Haus offices or your personal workshop?"

Dallas slipped onto the bar stool beside her and bit into his toast. "I thought I'd work out of your home office. Try to work up a few designs to present to Einar. You don't mind, do you?"

"Of course not. This is your home, too," she said, meaning it.

Dallas had been gracious enough to move into her house, despite the fact that his office and personal workshop were back at his place. That meant he had to commute there now rather than just traveling a few feet away from his bed when he arose in the morning.

"Will you be home for dinner?" Dallas sipped his coffee.

Okay, maybe it did still feel a little weird that this was now Dallas's home, too. That she had to share her personal space and navigate her way around his things—like the clothing he'd fold and lay on top of the hamper.

"Yes, dear." She flashed him a teasing smile. "I'll be home in time for dinner."

Dallas arranged the ingredients on Zora's kitchen counter to make his spicy chili and sweet jalapeño cornbread—a meal he knew Zora loved. He'd made it for her a few times when she'd come to his place for a movie night or to watch college basketball during March Madness.

He'd spent all morning at a secondary desk in Zora's home office, working on a few design ideas to present to Einar. However, the real point of the project was for Dallas to immerse himself in Icelandic life for several months and allow the place, the people and their furniture aesthetic to inspire him to create something fresh and new. Designs that represented a true blend of cultures.

This deal was important to him. He wanted to show Einar Austarsson that he was serious about the project and ready to set the wheels of the deal in motion. These kinds of projects typically took six months to a year of planning before he got on a plane and ventured abroad to what would be his temporary home.

Much like this one.

Dallas glanced around Zora's kitchen. It was sleek and modern with every fancy countertop appliance one could imagine: a spiralizer, an air fryer, an electric pressure cooker and a stand mixer. It was the exact opposite of the simple kitchen back at his cabin, once owned by his grandfather.

His place was small and dated. The kitchen was less than half the size of Zora's with limited usable counter space. But the cabin reminded him of his late grandfather and all the things the old man had taught him: like how to make five-alarm chili and how to design and build furniture. Growing up, it had been a hobby into which he'd poured his anger and frustration. It had evolved from a calling that brought him peace and satisfaction to a livelihood for himself and the people he employed here in Magnolia Lake and around the world.

Dallas rummaged through the cabinets in search of a pot suitable for making chili. He groaned quietly as he thought of his and Zora's conversation earlier that morning.

*You like saying that word, don't you?*

It obviously still made Zora uncomfortable for him to refer to her as his wife, though that's exactly what she was. He, on the other hand, felt a little thrill every time he said the word.

Zora Abbott Hamilton was his wife. And he'd been enjoying every minute of it. From the moment they'd awakened in bed together in that hotel in Vegas to talking about their plans for the day over breakfast that morning.

He loved that, at least for a little while, he got to share a life and a bed with this beautiful woman who had always meant so much to him and always would. So hell yeah, he liked calling Zora his wife.

He'd offered to father Zora's child because his friend desperately wanted to be a mother, and she meant the world to him. So he wanted to make motherhood happen for her. But his perspective had taken a sharp turn when he'd held Remi in his arms for the first time. Then, just to seal the deal, little Davis had offered to become Uncle Dallas's new best friend.

Dallas smiled fondly, thinking of the kids. That was

the night he'd realized that he, too, longed for a family. But he hadn't allowed himself to dwell on the thought before. Because marriages and relationships in the Hamilton family didn't seem to last.

So Dallas hadn't been eager to get married or have children. One failed relationship after another only confirmed his suspicions that he was better off as a bachelor. As long as he'd had Zora in his life, the fleeting nature of his romantic entanglements hadn't really mattered. But what he hadn't considered was that he and Zora were in a long-term relationship. One that was solid and had stood the test of time.

Why should their marriage be any different?

They loved each other, enjoyed each other's company, wanted the best for each other and were clearly sexually compatible. Having a child together would only strengthen the bond they already shared.

*So why not make it permanent?*

Dallas should've been unnerved by the idea of making this marriage a permanent one. But the idea had been building in his head and his heart from the moment he'd found that marriage certificate on his dresser at the hotel in Vegas.

He'd long wondered if the friendship that he and Zora had could become something more. And now he believed that it could—a thought that was thrilling and terrifying.

If it worked, they'd have the best of both worlds, being friends and lovers. If it didn't, he'd lose the woman who meant everything to him. It was the reason neither of them had wanted to risk getting involved. But now that he had a taste of what life could be like for them as lovers and friends, he couldn't imagine them not being both.

Dallas set a Dutch oven on the stove and rubbed at his chest. The thought of walking away from Zora a year from now caused an ache deep in his chest. Because he did love his best friend. And because they belonged together.

Now he just needed to figure out how to convince Zora of that.

# Nineteen

Zora lay in bed with Dallas on Sunday morning, her cheek pressed to his chest and one arm wrapped around his waist. She'd returned from her trip to Atlanta on Friday afternoon, and from the moment he'd picked her up at the airport, she'd been in heaven.

The kiss he'd greeted her with had turned her inside out and left her knees quivering and her body aching for him. As soon as they'd arrived back at her place, he'd been all too happy to oblige.

They'd spent the weekend making up for lost time, since Dallas would be leaving the next day for a trip to London.

Zora's phone suddenly began to play "A Song for Mama" by Boyz II Men—the custom ring for her mother.

She groaned, snuggling closer to her husband. Zora's

muscles felt warm and languid. Too relaxed and loose for her to reach all the way to the nightstand where her phone was perched.

"I'll call her back as soon as we get up," Zora murmured into his chest. Since neither of them seemed to have plans to get out of bed any time soon, she had no idea when that might be.

"Good, because I'm not done with you yet." Dallas grinned, rolling over onto her and kissing her mouth, his hardened length pressed against her.

Boyz II Men started to sing again.

"Ugh." Zora huffed, exasperated. Why hadn't she turned on her Do Not Disturb mode? "If I don't answer the phone, she'll think we're having sex."

"Good." Dallas trailed kisses down her neck. "Because we are."

"They don't need to know that."

"I'm pretty sure they already do." He chuckled, the sound of his voice warm and soothing, like warm honey poured over her skin. "We're newlyweds. It's safe to assume that they expect us to be fucking like rabbits."

"How very poetic." She jabbed him playfully in his hard belly.

Dallas kissed her neck. "You know I love your family, right?"

The muscles in Zora's back tensed. No conversation with a lover that began with that line ever ended well.

"Yeah?" Zora knew that Dallas loved her family. Still, the word came out as more of a question. "But?"

He gave her a knowing smile, his brown eyes twinkling. "You've only been home a few days, and I'm leaving tomorrow morning."

He brushed the hair from her face and pressed his

mouth to hers in a lingering kiss. Then he kissed her ear before whispering in a gruff, sexy voice, "So I'd much rather spend my last few hours here, making love to my wife."

He caressed her back and nibbled on her ear.

Zora shivered, her nipples stiffening as electricity traveled down her spine and settled into the damp, warm space between her thighs.

"Your *fake* wife," she murmured. Because, of course, she couldn't help herself. The moment between them felt so damn perfect and too damn *real*.

Dallas pulled back and studied her face. A devious smile curved one edge of his mouth. "But the orgasms I'm going to give her will be very, very real."

*Let the church say amen.*

She swallowed roughly, her heart racing. Her sex throbbed with the memory of how real every orgasm that he'd given her thus far had been.

Hell yes, she wanted more of that. But she also didn't want to seem too eager. To come off as desperate.

"This isn't just about my family. It's about your mom, too. Tish misses you. More than she's willing to admit." Zora stroked his cheek, his whiskers tickling her hand. "And it's just a few hours. We won't stay long. I promise."

"Okay." Dallas sighed. Despite the tiny smile he managed, there was a look of defeat in his brown eyes. He kissed her palm.

Dallas's romantic gesture made her heart flutter. She buried her cheek in his chest again, cradling her body against his. Zora had never felt so safe and content in a relationship. She could be herself with Dallas without judgment. She loved it, and she loved him. Still, none of this was the way she'd imagined finding and falling in love with the man she'd spend forever with.

There had been no stars in her eyes, no moment when they'd glanced at each other and realized they were hopelessly in love. Zora had been waiting for her epic love story and breathtaking romance her entire life. She wouldn't settle for this thing with Dallas because it was comfortable for both of them.

She wanted fireworks, and Dallas deserved them, too. Because he was an incredible man who would one day make someone a fantastic husband.

She wouldn't take that moment away from either of them. Nor would she risk losing her best friend forever when one or both of them eventually realized that they were better off as friends.

"Zora, Dallas, hello. I'm glad to see you two, because Tish and I have a million questions to ask you about the wedding," Zora's mother said as she and Dallas walked into her parents' kitchen, hand in hand.

"The wedding?" Zora repeated the words as if she hadn't heard them. A stalling tactic she'd used since she was a kid.

"Yes, Zora. The wedding we're planning for you here. You know, the one where your families actually get to attend." Her mother exchanged a look with Tish, not bothering to hide the bite of sarcasm in her voice.

They were definitely still not over the hurt of being absent from her and Dallas's wedding.

Dallas squeezed Zora's hand. "Of course, Ir—" He quickly shifted in the middle of saying her mother's name when the woman pointed at him, one brow raised. *"Mom,"* he said instead with a soft smile. "You two have been very patient, giving us time to acclimate to married life these past few weeks."

"But we need to ask you to be patient for just a little while longer," Zora interrupted, rubbing her husband's arm. "Dallas is leaving for London in the morning. We'll probably head out soon after dinner—so that he can get packed," she added quickly when both women cackled deviously.

Zora's cheeks heated. It wasn't as if her mother wasn't fully aware that she was a grown woman with a healthy sex life. Still, it felt odd hearing their mothers imply they were leaving dinner early expressly to have sex. Especially since it was true.

"I think the travel should slow down for both of us in a couple of weeks…at least for a bit," Dallas volunteered, filling the awkward moment. "Then we'll all sit down and plan everything out."

"Fine." Tish pointed a finger at the two of them. "But let's not put this off so long that your first child ends up being the flower girl at the wedding."

"Amen." Zora's mother laughed. "Now Dallas, why don't you join the boys in the den? Zora, Quinn stepped away for a minute, but she insisted on handling the cooking today. I'm sure she'd love your help preparing the fruit salad."

"Absolutely, Mom. I'll be right back."

Zora walked with Dallas toward the den.

"You all right, babe?" He stopped suddenly and settled his large hands on her waist, leaning down to give her a quick kiss on the lips.

Zora reminded herself that this was all one big show. As much for themselves as for her family. But damn if it didn't feel every bit as real as the solid chest her hands were pressed against and the soft, firm lips pressed to her own.

"I'm fine. But I promised you we wouldn't stay long, and I intend to keep that promise." She smacked him on his jeans-clad bottom. "You should go ahead. I'll be in later to say hello to everyone."

Dallas nodded, reluctantly releasing her after planting another kiss on her forehead.

Zora sucked in a deep breath, her eyes drifting closed for a moment.

"This isn't supposed to feel so…real," she whispered to herself. But she'd evidently said the words louder than she'd thought.

"What isn't supposed to feel real?" Quinn asked, emerging from the guest bathroom.

"Uh… I…" Zora swallowed. "Nothing, I was just talking to myself."

She quickly turned on her heels and returned to the kitchen with Quinn, her heart racing. Zora washed her hands at the sink, then dried them.

"Where do you want me to start?"

"Help me make the potato salad first?" Quinn asked.

"Of course." Zora stepped aside while Quinn drained the potatoes.

As they worked together in the kitchen, her friend was unusually quiet. Once the potato salad was finished, Quinn laid out pineapples, mangoes, apples, strawberries and blueberries for the fruit salad.

"Is everything okay, Quinn?" Zora asked. "Did something happen between you and Max?"

"No." Quinn waved a hand. "Max and I are fine."

"But something is bothering you," Zora hedged.

Though their grandfathers had been close friends for

decades, Zora and Quinn hadn't become friends until Quinn had come to work on a project for their family's company. And she couldn't be more thrilled that Quinn and her brother Max were together now. They were perfect for each other.

Quinn turned toward her. "I just wondered…this whole deal with you and Dallas…is this about—" Quinn looked around the space and stepped closer, lowering her voice "—that thing we talked about at the Magnolia Café that day. You know, when we ran into Sloane, Benji and the twins?"

*Shit.*

Zora gritted her teeth, groaning quietly. Other than Dallas, Quinn was the one person Zora had told about her interest in having a child on her own. At the time, Quinn and Max hadn't even been dating and she honestly didn't even know Quinn that well. But Quinn had been kind and easy to talk to, and the honest admission had just slipped out.

Zora had made the other woman promise not to say anything to her brother or anyone else about it. She'd obviously kept her word, or Max would've confronted her about it the moment he'd learned that she and Dallas were suddenly married.

"I don't want to lie to you, Quinn." Zora grabbed one of the pineapples, turned it on its side and picked up the chef's knife. "But I don't want to put you in a position where you're forced to either lie to my brother or—"

"I get it." Quinn held up a hand. "Enough said." She started peeling one of the mangoes. They worked in silence for a few moments before Quinn spoke again. "And you should know that I'm absolutely not judging here. Dallas is a great guy, and I've always thought you two behaved like a couple anyway. So you getting together didn't surprise me, Savannah, Kayleigh or either of your moms."

Zora stopped slicing the pineapple and turned to Quinn. "Why do I feel like there's a big fat *but* coming?"

Quinn shrugged. "It's not a *but* exactly. It's just something to keep in mind. That's all."

"Okay. I'm intrigued. Let's hear it." Zora put down the knife and wiped her hands on a kitchen towel. "What's wrong?"

"I don't know what arrangements you two have made, how permanent this thing is or if you're even really married—"

"Trust me," Zora said, "we definitely are."

Quinn returned to peeling and slicing the mango, her eyes on the cutting board.

"I couldn't help noticing the look on Dallas's face when you two are together." Her mouth curved in a soft smile. "There's no faking that kind of adoration, Zora. Whatever this is to you, to Dallas, this is plenty real."

Zora's cheeks tightened with an involuntary smile. "We've been best friends since we were kids," she said. "I adore him, too."

"No, sweetie," Quinn said in a distinct bless-your-li'l-heart voice. She set down her knife, dried her hands on the towel and put a hand on Zora's shoulder. "I'm talking head over heels in love here."

Zora cleared her throat. "Of course, we love each other. We've been best friends forever. But that's not the same as being *in love*."

"What do you think being in love is, Zora? To me, it's friendship with someone who truly gets you. Someone who always knows just what to say to make you smile when you've had a horrible day. Sex and attraction… that's the easy part. For some people it happens right away. For others, it happens so gradually you hardly realize it. But the friendship, mutual respect and really *knowing* each other…that's the hard stuff. That's what the rest of us struggle with. But you and Dallas already have that. You've had it nearly your entire lives."

"If my best friend was a woman, would you think we were soul mates?" Zora tipped her chin defiantly.

"If the two of you were as into each other as you and Dallas are…*absolutely*," Quinn said without hesitation. "Love is love, sweetie. And what you two have is *definitely* love."

Zora wrapped her arms around herself as she considered her friend's words.

"I know how important Dal's friendship is to you, Zora. So just make sure that you're both honest about your expectations for this marriage. Friendships like the one you two share are rare and worth saving." Quinn huffed, as if relieved. "That's it. That's all I wanted to say, and now that I have, I feel much better."

Quinn returned to slicing up the mango, and Zora went back to cutting the rough, spiky skin off the pineapple.

*Great.*

At least one of them felt better. Because now all Zora could think about was whether Quinn was right.

Was Dallas in love with her?

And if he was, what would happen to their friendship once their arrangement came to an end?

# Twenty

It had been two months since Dallas had awakened in Vegas to discover that he was now married to his best friend. Yet it barely seemed that long. And the whole thing felt more like an elaborate game of tag than a marriage.

If they were lucky, they got to spend a few days together before one or both of them had to jet off on some business-related trip. Most of the trips had been planned long before they'd gotten married and decided to start trying to have a baby. Still, he hated that they spent so much of their time apart. Zora had only agreed to stay married for one year, and he'd been silently building a case for making their marriage a permanent one. Trying to show her how much better their lives were now that they were together.

But whenever it seemed that Zora might be more open to the proposal, she'd say or do something to remind them both of the temporary nature of their relationship.

Dallas rubbed the last of the ebony stain into the cherrywood of the chaise longue he'd been working on for the past week. It was the final piece of a collection that he'd been inspired to create since he and Zora had been together. Initially, Dallas had hoped to design a few pieces to present to Einar. But instead he'd been inspired to create a line of sleek, modern furniture with a little bit of an edge. A series of pieces that lived comfortably in the space between masculine and feminine. The perfect compromise between his and Zora's styles.

He'd been inspired by the design of her office with its mix of masculine and feminine pieces and a dramatic black accent wall dotted with bright pops of white in floating shelves and matte-framed black-and-white photos of landscapes and of her family. There were even a few photos of the two of them on their many travels together.

None of this had been in his plans. But once the idea had seeped into his brain, he hadn't been able to stop obsessing over it. He'd made two different headboards, a bed frame and an office desk so far. But this chaise, which he envisioned as the perfect piece of furniture for the foot of Zora's bed, was the pièce de résistance of the entire line. And he couldn't wait to show her.

Dallas wiped his hands on a rag and stood back to admire his work. One more coat of the stain, plus a top coat to give it a shine. Then he would show the piece to his wife—the woman who'd inspired it.

His phone rang, and he glanced over at it on a nearby work surface. He was hoping it was Zora, but he quickly remembered that she'd taken his phone and set up a custom ring for herself. Dallas chuckled thinking of it.

It had been something she'd tried to get him to do for years and he'd never bothered. But now, as his wife, she'd grabbed his phone one night and set up custom rings for herself and for his mother.

He had to admit that it was damn useful. Since it was neither Zora nor his mother, he started to ignore the call. But when he stepped closer, he recognized the name on the lock screen.

*Einar Austarsson.*

Dallas's muscles tensed. Things had been crazy for Dallas the past few months. He and Einar had exchanged periodic emails about the project, but the man's slow responses had left Dallas wondering if Einar had changed his mind about collaborating.

He picked up the phone and answered, and the man greeted him cheerfully, as if they were old friends who'd lost touch. Einar explained that he'd been preoccupied with renovating their main warehouse after the roof collapsed during a particularly hard snowfall.

"But enough about that," Einar said cheerfully. "I'd like to accelerate our plans for collaboration. When can you join us here in Reykjavik?"

Dallas had anticipated this call for months, but he hadn't expected Einar to want to move so quickly.

His life had changed completely in two months. Dallas and Zora were married and actively trying to have a baby. And he was in a race against time.

He had ten months to convince the woman he loved that their marriage wasn't just a fluke. That they belonged together.

Zora got into her car and made her way out of the parking lot. She'd left work a few minutes early on a dark winter afternoon, eager to get home to her husband. Over the past few months of being married, both she and Dallas had floated in and out of town, making the most of the few days here or there that they got to spend together.

She and Dallas had yet to get pregnant, though certainly not for lack of trying. And while they'd both thoroughly enjoyed this new physical aspect of their relationship, they also just really enjoyed each other's company and this deeper level of intimacy. Even if all they were doing was sitting together in her office working on their respective projects or lying in bed binge-watching a show on Netflix.

As friends with busy lives, they'd gotten accustomed to not seeing each other for weeks or months at a time. But now Dallas's absence from her life, and from her bed, left her with a deep sense of emptiness and loss. This marriage was a friends-with-benefits deal with an expiration date—set by her. Dallas had dropped not so subtle hints that he'd be *content* to continue their arrangement.

Honestly? She was flattered—even thrilled—whenever Dallas joked that maybe they should just stay married. But what Dallas hadn't ever said was that he *loved* her or that he was *in love* with her. Being content with each other wasn't enough to sustain a marriage. They'd eventually come to resent each other the way his father had come to resent his mother. Because it seemed obvious that Douglas Hamilton hadn't ever really wanted to be married or have children.

What if their marriage, entered into in a hazy stupor neither of them could recall, turned out the same way?

The prospect of losing the friendship they'd nurtured since childhood broke her heart.

As Zora waved good night to the guard at the gate, the opening notes from Ed Sheeran's "Castle on the Hill" rang from her purse.

*Dallas's custom ringtone.*

"Hey," she said. "I was just about to call to see if I should grab dinner on the way home."

He chuckled. "Is that your way of asking if I've cooked dinner?"

Zora couldn't help laughing, too. "Busted. I'm sorry, but you've spoiled me with the delicious meals you make whenever you're home. I think I'm going to miss that most," she teased.

"Oh, it's my cooking you're going to miss the most, huh?" He laughed. "Then maybe I need to step up my game tonight."

"Ooh." The word slipped out of Zora's mouth before she realized it. Her nipples beaded at the prospect. "That sounds…promising. I can't wait to get home."

"Good." Dallas's rich, husky laugh rang throughout the car. "But first, can you make a detour and come to the cabin? I want to show you what I've been working on the past few months."

"Tonight?" She hadn't intended to sound so whiny, but it was a Friday night at the end of what had been a long week, and she was physically and mentally exhausted.

"It'll be worth it. I promise." She could hear the soft smile in her husband's voice. "Got a surprise for you."

"Really?" Zora perked up, thoroughly intrigued.

She'd spent the past few hours dreaming of a hot bath and a warm meal—even if it was just a cup of ramen noodles heated in the microwave. This cold winter night was made for her warmest pj's and a pair of fuzzy pink slippers. But Dallas sounded so excited.

How could she possibly say no?

He'd rearranged his entire life to give her the child she so desperately wanted. The very least she could do was stop by his workshop to see whatever it was he wanted to show her.

"On my way," she confirmed with a smile. Zora was unbelievably grateful to Dallas, but also a little uneasy with how quickly she felt a sense of obligation.

A few minutes later, her phone rang again. Zora answered it.

*"Gott kvöld,* Brigitta. *Hvernig hefur þú það?"* Zora used the limited Icelandic her friend had taught her to wish the woman a good evening and ask how she was.

Zora hadn't spoken to Brigitta in some time, but they frequently exchanged emails. And over the past few months, Zora had done some speaking engagements and mentored women with the potential to be future business executives. All of which had been coordinated by the international women's organization Brigitta sat on the board of.

It had been Dallas who'd championed her to Brigitta as a potential speaker and mentor. Zora knew firsthand that there was a dearth of women in high-level positions in corporations. Still, she'd been reluctant to take on a volunteer role with the organization at first.

Dallas had encouraged her with stories of the fulfilling work he'd done with native artists around the world. Many of whom were women who were the primary earners in their families. Dallas reminded Zora that she could have a powerful impact on those women because she understood how tough it could be for women who did manage to achieve executive-level positions.

Zora was glad that she'd taken on the challenge.

Her volunteer work through Brigitta's organization had given Zora a deep sense of joy and renewed purpose in her work. It was something she hoped to do more of. And it had her thinking deeply about ways to expand King's Finest's community involvement.

"I am well," Brigitta said, the usual lilt absent from her new friend's voice. "But I think that there is something you should know."

Zora heaved a sigh, trying to put the uneasiness of her call with Brigitta out of her head for the moment. She drove down the narrow road that led to Dallas's cabin and pulled into the long driveway.

The cabin itself was modest. Dallas had done some basic updates but had yet to give the place the renovation it needed. However, he had renovated the space that meant the most to him—the large barn on the property. That was where he spent most of his time when he was home.

She got out of the car and made her way toward the barn. Dallas slid the door open and greeted her with *that* smile. The one that lit his eyes and animated his entire face. The smile that instantly made her feel better. Appreciated. *Loved.*

In that moment, all of the doubt, fear and hesitation she had about being married to her best friend seemed to fade away. Maybe he hadn't said the words explicitly. But for the first time it seemed so very clear. He loved her, and not just as a friend.

"Hey, beautiful." He kissed her. "How was your day?"

"Better now that I'm here with you." She returned his smile.

The moments they spent together made her incredibly happy. But it wasn't just her day that was better by being with him. Her life was so much better with Dallas Hamilton in it as her husband.

An involuntary grin slid across Dallas's face. Zora's words filled him with an indescribable sense of satisfaction. Because his days and nights were better with her in them, too.

He could stand there all night with his gorgeous wife in his arms, but the temperature had started to drop and despite the wool coat that Zora was wearing, she was shivering.

Dallas rubbed his wife's arm, then escorted her inside his workshop, sliding the barn door back into place behind them.

Mostly, it was a place of peace and creativity for him. Designing and building each piece of furniture was a form of moving meditation for Dallas—as yoga was for some people. And he was surrounded by memories of his grandfather, who had taken him under his wing and taught him the art and craft of building unique furniture that reflected the place from which it came and the people he was building it for.

"So many memories here." Zora squeezed his hand as she glanced around the space. "I miss your grandfather."

It was as if she was somehow inside his head, as she so often was. Because she understood him more than any other person on this earth. And he understood her, too.

Dallas nodded, breathing through the emotions that choked back his words.

"So...you wanted to show me something?" Zora asked brightly.

"Yeah." Dallas shoved his hands in his pockets, his stomach suddenly taking a dip, as it did on those damned roller coasters his friend loved so much.

He swallowed hard, nervous to show her what he'd been working on. Dallas had always shared his work with his friend at every stage of production. He valued her feedback on his projects, even if he didn't always agree. But this collection felt more personal than anything he'd created before.

If Zora hated it, the rejection would cut much deeper this time. Because he'd poured his heart and soul into each piece.

"It's over here." Dallas led Zora to a far corner of the workshop. He indicated the sleek, black leather chaise that he'd finished earlier that day. It was the final piece of the new collection that he'd designed. He tipped his chin in the direction of the piece and shoved his hands in his pockets. "What do you think?"

"Oh my God, Dallas." Zora ran her fingertips over the buttery-soft leather—a material he hadn't often incorporated into his designs. "This just might be the sexiest piece of furniture I've ever seen in my life." Zora walked around the chaise, her hand never leaving its surface. "You know I love everything you make. But this is stunning. It's my absolute favorite piece that you've made."

"I'm glad you like it, Zo." Dallas sighed in quiet relief, his heart expanding in his chest. "Because you were my inspiration."

"Me?" Her eyes widened as she looked at him, then returned her attention to the chaise, as if seeing it for the first time.

"Yes." Dallas glided a hand over the surface, but his gaze was on Zora. "It's bold and sleek. Contemporary with a bit of an edge. Curvy, sexy as hell and…"

"Unapologetically Black?" She grinned, her eyes sparkling.

Dallas chuckled. "Actually, I chose the color because it's one of your favorites and it fits with your current design scheme."

"You made the chaise for me?" Zora pressed a hand to her chest.

After all the intimate moments they'd shared, it was *this*—revealing how much she moved and inspired him—that made him feel most vulnerable. "I thought it would look nice at the foot of your bed. Or maybe it could replace the chair you hate in the seating area near the window."

"So there'd be room for both of us to sit and read?" Her eyes glistened when she met his gaze.

"Something like that." He smiled.

"Thank you, Dal. I love it. It's beautiful."

"So are you." He cradled her wet cheek and grazed her lower lip with his thumb before claiming her mouth with a kiss.

Zora smiled sheepishly, tucking her hair behind her ear. "And what about these?" She indicated the bed frame, dresser and bedside table nearby.

"Initially, it was just the chaise that came to mind." Dallas rubbed his neck. "Then I decided to make a few pieces to go with it. Do you like them?" Dallas ran his hand over the high-gloss finish of the cherrywood stained ebony.

"I do. They're a perfect complement to the chaise. It's a little bit of a departure from your usual style, but I love it, Dallas. Are these pieces prototypes for Einar?"

"No." He shifted his gaze from hers. They'd talk about that later. He cleared his throat. "I'd started out with that intention, and then it just morphed into something that felt too personal for a collaboration." Dallas shrugged. "I'm adding it to the Hamilton Haus lineup. I'd like to call the collection Zora."

Her gaze snapped to his and she blinked. "You're naming the collection after me?"

"If you're okay with it." Dallas dragged a hand through his hair, suddenly feeling self-conscious. "I thought I should run it by you fir—"

Before he could finish his sentence, Zora had stepped forward and cradled his face in her hands, her eyes drifted shut as she pressed her mouth to his.

Dallas slipped his arms around Zora's waist beneath the tan coat and pulled her tight against him. He relished the sensation of the generous curves that had inspired him as Zora's body melded into him, her lush lips gliding over his. He tilted her head back, slipping his tongue inside the warm cavern of her mouth—minty and sweet.

Despite the chill in the winter air outside, Dallas's face burned, and a fire ignited in his belly as the heat built between them, consuming them. Making him hungry with desire for the incredible woman who'd been his wife for the past two months.

Maybe their marriage had been the result of a series of mistakes and questionable choices, but he was damn glad it had happened. That he got to be Zora Abbott Hamilton's husband. That she was wearing his ring and—at least for now—had appended his last name to hers. And he would do whatever it took to show her that the marriage wasn't a mistake.

It was destiny. Written in the stars the moment they'd encountered each other on that playground twenty-five years ago.

As their kiss grew more intense, his body ached with its need for hers. Zora was so incredibly sexy. Something that he'd tried his best to ignore for the past ten years. But now he didn't have to pretend not to notice what a beautiful goddess his best friend was. Or that she had a body that could stop traffic. And there could be no more convincing himself that they were better off as friends.

But he was on the clock. He needed to convince Zora that they belonged together, even if it was a ridiculous fluke that had brought them to this point.

Without breaking their heated kiss, Dallas slipped the coat from Zora's shoulders, dropping it onto a nearby bench. She yanked up his T-shirt, and he helped her tug the garment over his head, tossing it onto the floor. It was quickly joined by her suit and blouse and his jeans. Finally, they stripped each other of their underwear, which joined the quickly growing pile on the floor.

Dallas broke their kiss, leading Zora to the chaise and bending her over it, preparing to enter her from behind. It was one of the positions Zora had identified as being ideal for conception. But his wife turned to him, an impish glint in her eye as she pushed him down onto the chaise and climbed onto his lap, facing him.

Zora wrapped her legs around him, locking them behind his back and she looped her arms around his neck.

"I like it," he murmured between kisses. "But I thought we were focusing on positions ideal for conception."

"I know." Zora stroked his cheek, her eyes searching his. "But tonight... I don't want it to be about us trying to get pregnant. I just want this to be about...us."

Dallas nodded, his heart squeezing in his chest at the implication that Zora was finally admitting what he'd already known for months. That what they shared went deeper than their temporary arrangement or even their wish to have a child together.

Dallas wrapped one arm around Zora's waist as he pulled her closer, the slick space between her thighs gliding along his hardened length.

Zora murmured with pleasure at the sensation of the stiff bundle of nerves grinding against his steely length. Her breath came in short, throaty pants, both of them gasping for air at the feverish kiss.

He gripped her hips, his fingers digging into her soft flesh as he lifted her, guiding her onto his aching member. He was desperate to be inside her again, as if they hadn't made love earlier that morning. She reached for his hardened dick, pumping it with her hand before guiding it inside her. Zora glided down onto him, and they both groaned with pleasure.

"Fuck, Zora." He whispered into her hair, "Babe, you feel so damn amazing."

Zora kissed him, her thumbs pressed to his cheeks as her lips clashed with his. Her hips moved slowly at first. But as the intensity of their kiss escalated, the movement of her hips mirrored their frantic kiss.

Zora cried out his name, her body going stiff as she held on to his shoulders tightly, as if she needed his support. He tightened his grip on her thighs, hoping he wouldn't leave bruises as he moved against her.

His body was suddenly racked with the deepest, most intense pleasure. He wrapped her in his arms and buried his face in her hair, which smelled like some sweet chocolate confection.

"Zora, I love you." His voice was low, the words barely more than a whisper. Words Dallas had wanted to say for months. But he could never seem to find the right time to say them.

Zora didn't move. Didn't speak. It felt as if she was barely breathing.

The silence between them rang in his ears, as loud as the circular saw of his grandfather's he'd used to make the chaise they were on. Dallas shut his eyes closed and sighed.

The awkward silence loomed over them like some invisible monster that had climbed from beneath the chaise the moment he'd opened his stupid mouth and told her he loved her.

But it was true; he did love her. And not just as a friend. It had never been clearer to him. But he suspected that his sudden declaration of love had freaked Zora out.

Zora climbed off him, stepped into her shearling-lined suede boots and slipped on her coat. She wrapped it around her, as if she needed a shield between them. She quickly stooped to gather her clothing.

"Bathroom," she called over her shoulder as she hurried in that direction.

Dallas sighed, a knot twisting in his gut.

*That didn't go how I'd hoped.*

"Meet me over at the cabin, Zo. I'll order something for dinner. Then we can…talk," Dallas called after her.

Zora stopped in her tracks, as if she'd suddenly run into a wall. She glanced back at him over her shoulder and nodded before resuming her retreat.

Dallas shrugged on his jeans and shirt and grabbed up his belt and underwear, not bothering to put either on. Then he stuck his feet into his boots without tying them and headed to the cabin to order dinner and shower.

His wife had evidently been unsettled by his admission of love. But he meant every word, and he was certain she felt the same.

Dallas groaned, feeling temporarily defeated, yet determined to make Zora see that what they had was real and worth fighting for.

# Twenty-One

Zora shut the bathroom door behind her, instantly furious at herself for running away like a child. Awkward moments like this were exactly why she'd been so terrified of taking on marriage and parenthood with her best friend.

Did she love him? *Hell yes.* But before Vegas, it had been so easy to delineate the *type* of love she had for Dallas.

Zora had always admired that the ancient Greeks understood how truly complicated love was. They had four words for it: *agape* was love of mankind, *storge* was the love parents had for their children, *philia* was love between friends and *eros* was passionate, erotic love.

BV—in the time Before Vegas—it had been clear that the love they shared was a love between friends, pure and simple. And she'd really, *really* intended to keep it that way. Even after they'd agreed to have a child together. But little by little, things had been shifting between them over the past few months. Their marriage was starting to feel less and less like an arrangement and more like it was real. Like the love they shared was so much deeper than friendship or even just sex.

Had she fallen in love with her best friend? Was he in love with her, as Quinn believed? Zora had been wrestling with all those thoughts in her head, but she hadn't wanted to say them out loud—not even to herself. So she hadn't been ready to hear them coming from her best friend.

Zora plopped down on the cold toilet seat. She was an accomplished exec who mentored other career women, a candidate for CEO of her company and on the precipice of beginning the journey into motherhood. So she needed to have a grown-up conversation with her husband about what he'd said and her growing, complicated feelings for him.

She would clean up, put on her coat and traipse over to the cabin to have the conversation she'd been terrified of having for the past few weeks.

Zora's keys jingled in her pocket as she clutched her clothing in one hand and pulled the tan wool coat tightly around her naked body with the other. She set her things on the counter and surveyed the space.

While Dallas had overhauled the barn, he'd only made a few improvements to the cabin. Still, what he'd done had been a dramatic improvement to the dark, dank space it once was.

A stunning billiard table that Dallas had built himself dominated the sparsely furnished open area in the center of the cabin. The hallway on the left led to the master bedroom. The hallway on the right led to Dallas's office and a small guest room.

Dallas had brought Cole's company in to open up the back wall of the cabin and install large windows that let in lots of light. Her brother had also revamped and modernized the small kitchen so it could accommodate a dishwasher, a beer fridge and a full-size, state-of-the-art refrigerator.

Dallas had crafted the gorgeous slab of wood that served as the island countertop himself. Made from salvaged, old-growth redwood with a live edge, it served as the breakfast bar and provided the kitchen's only real food prep workspace.

Still clutching the coat closed with one hand, Zora made her way to the master bedroom, where she could hear the shower running. She sucked in a deep breath, dropped her clothing and the coat onto Dallas's bed, toed off her fur-lined boots, and padded into the bathroom.

Dallas stood beneath the shower, rinsing shampoo from his hair. Zora opened the glass door and stepped inside, startling him momentarily.

He cocked his head and a slow smirk lifted one corner of his sensual mouth. "So the shower crashing, that's your thing now, huh?"

"Maybe." She shrugged, reining in a smile. "Is it a problem?"

"Hell no." Dallas wrapped an arm around her waist. "You can shower with me any time, Mrs. Hamilton." He leaned down and kissed her mouth.

"That's Ms. Abbott-Hamilton." Zora kissed him again. "But because you're cute and you're definitely packing—" she pressed her body against his steely length "—I'm gonna let it slide."

Dallas chuckled, his laughter bouncing off the tiled walls.

"Are we all right, Zo?" He studied her face as he held her in his arms. "You seemed pretty upset about me saying—"

"I know, and I'm sorry." She cut him off before he could repeat the words. The muscles in her neck and back tensed as warm water beat on their bodies. "I was just…stunned to hear you say the words."

"I meant what I said, Zo." He caressed her cheek, his gaze soft and warm. "I love you, and not just as a friend. I love being your husband. Love the prospect of being a father to our kids. I love that you're both my best friend and the woman who has my heart and always will."

Zora furrowed her brows, her heart breaking. Dallas wasn't making what she had to say easier. Zora swallowed hard, the words caught in her throat. She tucked wet curls behind her ear.

Her voice was shaky. "Dallas, I—"

"I love you, Zora," he said again. "And I want to be with you. Not just for a few more months. What we have… I want this forever, and I know you do, too."

She did. Zora realized that now. But she also realized that this arrangement wasn't fair to Dallas. Maybe they were meant to be together. But perhaps it just wasn't the right time in their lives.

"Dallas, I don't think that—" Zora tried to drop her gaze, but he maintained his light grip on her chin, as if this connection between them was a lifeline he was holding on to at all costs.

"It's true, Zo. This isn't me getting caught up in my

feelings because the sex is amazing. It's how I genuinely feel. I might've been under the influence when I recited my wedding vows in that Vegas chapel. But, baby, I meant every single word. I love you, Zo. I think I always have." His voice wavered a little.

Zora closed her eyes, her eyelashes wet with tears. His sweet words and the emotion with which he delivered them made her heart squeeze in her chest.

She wanted to tell him the truth—that she loved him and wanted to be with him, too. But that wasn't what she'd come here to say. Because it wasn't what was best for the man she adored.

"Dallas, I love you, too," she said, tears streaming down her cheeks. His expression instantly went from joy to trepidation. Because he knew her well enough to know that she was gathering the strength to say something that pained her. "But this arrangement... I didn't realize how unfair it is to you."

"Shouldn't I be the one to decide whether or not I feel like this is unfair to me?"

"You're a good friend, Dal, and you've been an amazing husband—"

"I've *been* an amazing husband?" Dallas cocked one brow. "As in past tense?"

When fat tears rolled down her cheeks in response, his frown deepened.

Dallas turned off the water and stepped out of the shower. He handed her a towel, then grabbed one for himself before stalking into the bedroom.

Zora followed him into the other room, drying her wet skin with the soft white towel he'd handed her.

She sat at the foot of his bed, unsure of what to say.

Dallas rummaged through his drawers in silence

before finally grabbing a pair of boxers and slipping them on. He turned to her and sighed, dragging a hand through his hair.

"You're asking to end our marriage *now*, aren't you?"

"Yes." She whispered the word, her heart breaking.

"Why, Zo?" He sat beside her on the bed. "It clearly isn't what you want, and it isn't what I want either. What we've built…it means *everything* to me." He covered her trembling hand with his.

"It means everything to me too, Dal. But I'm scared." Zora wasn't accustomed to admitting her fears and weaknesses; not even to herself. They were emotions she stuffed deep down. Something to be overcome. Dallas intertwined their fingers and tightened his grip on her hand. Zora instantly felt a sense of comfort.

"I know that the prospect of us making this a real marriage makes the stakes much higher. And yes, that does seem terrifying, given what we have to lose," Dallas admitted. "You're not alone in that, Zo. I don't know exactly what this next chapter of our lives will bring, either. But I know that as long as we're together, it's going to be amazing, and that together we can get through anything."

"I want to believe that, Dal. I do, but—"

"I'm not asking you to believe in some fairy tale, Zo. I'm asking you to climb down into the trenches with me and fight for it, because this friendship is too important to us. Our past failed relationships couldn't compete with our jobs or our families. But you, Zora, are my priority. Your love, your friendship and the family that we're trying to make…they mean everything to me. For you, sweetheart, I'm willing to make sacrifices."

"Like your decision to pass on the collaboration with Einar Austarsson?" she asked.

Dallas's eyes widened. "How'd you…" He rubbed the back of his neck and sighed. "Brigitta told you."

It wasn't a question, so she didn't bother confirming what he clearly already knew.

"I didn't pass on the project," Dallas hedged. "I requested that we put it on the shelf for now."

"But why, Dallas?" She cradled his cheek. "You've worked so hard to put this collaboration in motion."

Dallas turned his head and kissed her palm. He sighed. "I thought we'd be moving forward on this in a few months, maybe a year. But he wanted me to come to Reykjavik as soon as possible to set things up. It would take about three months. I told him I couldn't commit to that right now because we're trying to start a family."

"What did he say?" Zora asked.

"He'd assumed you were coming, too." Dallas rubbed his chin and chuckled bitterly. "I reminded him that my wife is an executive who can't just pick up and move abroad for three months. So I passed on the deal for now and asked him to keep me in mind. Perhaps we can collaborate in some way down the road."

Her eyes filled with tears, and she squeezed his hand. "Honey, I can't believe you'd give up this deal for me. I know how important it is to you."

Dallas shrugged as if losing this opportunity, which could make his company millions and further expand his brand and reach, was no big deal. "Now you know that you're more important to me than working with Einar Austarsson or anything else."

Zora's heart felt full and as if it were ripping apart at the seams. "I appreciate the sacrifice you're willing to make for me, Dal. But I didn't and would never ask you to make such a sacrifice. I want what's best for you. I want you to be happy," she said. "All you've talked about is how much you wanted this."

"True." He squeezed her hand as he peered into her eyes. "But that was before I realized that I want to be with you. To make babies with you. To build a life with you right here in Magnolia Lake." A soft smile kissed his lips.

Dallas was saying all the right things. Pushing all the right buttons. Giving her *everything* she could ever ask of him.

At the expense of himself.

She couldn't let him do that.

"You didn't consult with me on this. You didn't even ask if I'd consider coming with you."

"And would you have, Zo?" he asked pointedly, then sighed, running a hand through his hair. "We both already know the answer to that."

"So you just decided for me?" She was genuinely hurt and angry.

"It's one project, Zora. Hamilton Haus is doing fine. This isn't the end of the world."

"These immersive projects you do every few years are an integral part of your brand. It's what makes Hamilton Haus so unique. More importantly, those projects make you immensely happy, Dal. And they do so much good for the native artists you feature from all over the world. I can't take that away from you."

"Marriage is about sacrifice, Zora." Dallas slipped his hand into her hair and stroked her cheek. "I'm willing to sacrifice that aspect of my business or at least adjust it."

"Marriage is about compromise," Zora countered. "Both sides have to give a little to find a happy medium. If only one person is making all the sacrifices, the relationship won't work. It'll cause resentment. I don't want that for us, Dal."

"So what are you saying, Zo?" The pained look on her husband's face broke her heart.

Tears started to flow down her face again. "I'm saying that as much as I want this, I'm not sure how to make this work for both of us."

"Zo, sweetheart, please just tell me what you want. Ask me anything." He leaned down, pressing his forehead to hers.

Zora sucked in a deep breath and closed her eyes. Then she opened them, forcing a smile, even through her tears, as her eyes searched his.

"Two things. First, tomorrow I want you to call Einar and tell him that you've changed your mind." She stroked his cheek.

Dallas nodded sadly, his eyes filled with the same pain she felt. "All right. What else?"

She loosened the towel, letting it fall away as she climbed onto his lap and pressed a kiss to his lips. "Make love to me."

Dallas kissed her and made love to her as if it was the last time they'd ever be together.

The possibility that it might be tore Zora apart.

But she loved Dallas too much to let him give up this opportunity. Regardless of what it might mean for the two of them.

# Twenty-Two

Zora stood at the front of the boardroom before her grandpa Joe—whose recovery from his stroke was going well; her father, Duke; and her brothers Blake, Parker and Max. She'd just laid out her case for establishing the King's Finest Foundation and proposed that she be the one to spearhead the project.

Dallas had been in Iceland for nearly two weeks. She'd spent many of those nights in tears as she lay alone in bed, staring at the ceiling and wishing her husband was there. But she'd spent some of her time productively, developing the proposal she'd just presented to her family.

Her father and grandfather liked the idea of starting a foundation that would do good in underserved communities, strengthen the KFD brand and cement their legacies. But her father had an expected question.

"If you're shifting your focus to establishing the foundation, who'll run sales?" He frowned, rubbing his whiskered chin. "I don't need to tell you how important your work here is, Zora."

"Thanks, Dad." She smiled. "My assistant, Emily, is smart and ambitious. She's been critical to the team since I hired her right out of college six years ago. Her talents are being vastly underutilized in her current role," Zora admitted, returning to her seat beside Max.

"In my volunteer work, I'm giving women the knowledge and tools to ascend the career ladder. Charity begins at home. I'm not suggesting Emily can take over for me. But I've given her increasing responsibilities, and she's exceeded my expectations every single time. I'm proposing that I only retain the highest-level tasks while dividing the rest between Emily—in a newly minted role with a commensurate title and salary—and two other members of the team who are also ready for more responsibility."

Zora folded her hands on the table and surveyed the faces of her family, who were also the company's executive board.

"Excellent plan, Zora." Her grandfather beamed. "I'm proud of you for putting this together. Inspired by the race to be CEO?"

"Actually, about that… I've given it a lot of thought, and I'm committed to the success of the foundation and to maintaining our forward momentum in sales. So I'd like to withdraw my name for consideration and endorse Blake."

The faces of everyone in the room conveyed various levels of shock. Not surprising. After all, she was the most competitive person at the table.

"This isn't a democracy and Blake isn't a political candidate, Zora," Parker pointed out. He looked especially agitated.

"No, it isn't," her father confirmed. "But family always comes first here at King's Finest. So your grandfather and I certainly care what you think. You'll be the nucleus of this company, working together long after we're gone. Your wishes carry weight."

"Good," Max said. "Because I've been doing a lot of thinking about this, too. Would I like to be the CEO? Sure. But I honestly do believe Blake is best suited for the position. So, I'd like to endorse Blake, too. Not because he's the firstborn. Because his knowledge, work ethic, temperament and the respect he's earned from everyone here at the company recommend him as the *logical* choice." Max smirked at Parker—Mr. Logic—when he stressed the word.

Parker twisted his mouth and groaned. "To be clear, I'm *not* withdrawing myself from consideration," Parker said. "But I acknowledge the logic behind your arguments. So if Blake is the person designated as the next CEO of King's Finest, I believe he'll represent the company well. And I'll do my part to support him."

Her father exchanged a look with their grandfather, who nodded.

"I'm glad you've come to this conclusion on your own," Duke said. "Because your grandfather and I agree that Blake should be the next CEO of King's Finest Distillery. You all put the interests of this family and our company ahead of your self-interests. And I couldn't be prouder." He beamed.

"Good job, brat." Max turned to Zora when the meeting ended. "By the way, I'm sorry I wasn't more receptive when you returned from Vegas married. You took us all by surprise, but you and Dallas are right for each other. Marriage looks good on you, Zo."

"Thanks, Max." Zora forced a smile. Their families knew that Dallas had gone to Reykjavik for business. They weren't aware that their relationship was in limbo. She'd gone to Sunday dinner, put on a brave face and updated their families on her husband's trip, based on their daily, early morning phone calls.

The only two people who seemed to truly realize how devastated she was over her separation from her husband were Cole and Quinn. But she hadn't confided the truth to either of them.

When she rose from her seat, Blake was there.

"Thanks, Zo." He hugged her. "That was unexpected, but I appreciate your confidence and support. How's the wedding planning coming?"

Zora groaned. "The moms are driving us crazy. But with Dallas in Reykjavik right now, I'm hoping they'll back off a bit."

"Be patient with them. They're over the moon about you and Dallas finally getting together," Blake said. He smiled. "We all are."

*Great.* Now her knucklehead brothers wanted to be supportive of her marriage to Dallas?

*Figures.*

"Hang in there with the wedding stuff, Zora." Parker patted her shoulder. "Besides, the more they're focused on your wedding, the less they're bothering Kayleigh and me about ours." Parker flashed a rare grin, and Zora couldn't help laughing, too.

It was the end of another long day, and she felt more than a little fatigued. She just wanted to go home, crawl under the covers, and think about how amazing her life had been those first months they were married. Wishing there was a way to make this marriage work for both of them.

# Twenty-Three

Zora stood in her mother's kitchen before Sunday dinner, staring out the window onto the backyard where her father manned the grill. Her heart ached and all she could think of was the last time Dallas had been here with the family.

She missed him more each day. So much that it felt like she was making herself physically ill. She was pretty sure she was coming down with something. Her mother had felt her forehead and informed her that she had a serious case of missing her man.

Zora was not amused.

She looked out the window at her mother, most of her siblings and their spouses, who'd donned jackets and braved the crisp late fall air to sit around the fire pit and keep her father company. Savannah and Kayleigh were in the family room with Remi, who was now three months old and getting bigger every day.

Maybe she was feeling especially somber because she and Emily were leaving the next day for their week-long trek across Europe to meet with distributors in Belgium, Finland, Sweden and Germany.

Zora was startled by the slamming of the fridge. She hadn't even heard Cole arrive.

"You plan on mooning over the dude the entire three months he'll be in Iceland having the time of his life?" Cole twisted the cap off his beer.

"That's it." Zora turned to her brother, one fist on her hip. "Everyone else in this family has accepted my relationship with Dallas. But you—the one person I *expected* to have my back—you've been a total jack-ass about it."

"Look, you don't need to get so upset about me razz-ing your little boyfriend—"

"Dal is *not* my boyfriend, Cole. He's my *husband*, and he's been practically a member of this family since we were kids. You two have always gotten along fine."

"I know," Cole said gruffly, then sipped his beer.

"Then what the hell is your problem?" She poked a finger into Cole's shoulder. "Why are you suddenly treating Dallas like the enemy? He isn't. He's the same amazing guy who's always been a friend to all of us." Zora's voice broke. Tears clogged her throat and stung her eyes. Wetness streaked down her cheeks, which made her furious with her brother and with herself.

Zora never wanted to be babied by her brothers. She wanted them to recognize that she was as smart and as tough as they were. So she'd learned long ago never to let them see her cry.

She was breaking her own code and she was livid about it.

Cole set down his beer and grasped her arm. "Zo, I'm sorry. I didn't mean to hurt your feelings."

"My feelings aren't hurt." Zora yanked her arm from her brother's grip and propped a fist on her hip. She tipped her chin, leveling her angry gaze at him. "I'm *furious*. You've never treated anyone else's spouse or partner this way. In fact, you adore Savannah, Kayleigh and Quinn. So why are you being so shitty to Dallas?"

Cole wrinkled his brow, picked up his beer and swigged it. He shrugged his shoulders in response to her question, which only infuriated her.

"That's bullshit, Cole. There has to be a reason you're behaving this way. What could possibly have changed in the few months since Dallas was here for Mom and Dad's anniversary and for Benji and Sloane's wedding? You two got along fine then."

"You really want to know?" Cole asked.

"Obviously." Zora glared at her brother.

"He lied to us." Cole set his beer down again. "He's always sworn there was nothing going on between you. Then suddenly, you two elope. That didn't come out of nowhere, Zora. Evidently, there was a lot more than friendship between you."

"*That's* why you're upset?" Zora could barely restrain a laugh. "Because you think we've been hooking up all this time and he lied to you about it?"

Cole folded his arms. His expression indicated that he didn't see the humor in the situation.

"First of all—" Zora pointed an accusatory finger at her brother "—it's none of your damn business who I have or haven't been sleeping with. Second—" she held up two fingers "—Dal didn't lie to you. We were never together before we got married." Zora relaxed against the kitchen counter, shrugging her shoulders. "Our decision to get married was spontaneous. It was as much of a surprise to us as it was to all of you. But it felt right and we were happy—"

"*Were*?" Cole raised an eyebrow. "As in you aren't anymore?"

"Are," she said. "I meant we *are* happy." But her eyes wouldn't cooperate, and tears spilled down her cheeks. She sniffled. "Why can't you just be happy for us, bucket head?" She shoved her brother's shoulder again.

Cole hugged her, despite her objections. Her tears and makeup were getting all over his dark shirt.

He pulled her away from the window so their family wouldn't see her crying.

"You're right. I was a jerk. But something about your story just wasn't right, so I was concerned. You're my little sister and my closest remaining friend," Cole said. "Guess I didn't take the sudden news of losing you, too, so well."

Zora wiped her face and stared at her brother.

*His closest remaining friend?*

Suddenly, the real issue became clear. Why hadn't she recognized it earlier?

"This isn't so much about me and Dal as it is about you and Quinn, right?" Her voice was tempered with compassion.

"I don't know what you're talking about." Cole averted his gaze from hers. He gripped the bottle and took a swig.

"Yes, you do," Zora said softly. She glanced around the kitchen to ensure no one else was around. Then she lowered her voice and stepped closer. "You're not as okay with Max and Quinn being together as you pretend, are you?"

Cole's frown deepened, his expression stony. "They're happy, and I'm happy for them."

"Then why do you look so wounded?" Zora placed a hand on her brother's arm. She studied his expression, though his eyes wouldn't meet hers. This wasn't simple jealousy or even resentment. "The friendship you and Quinn struck up… For her, it really was just that. But for you…what…did you think that after you'd gotten done sleeping your way across the South you two would eventually end up together?"

Cole glared at her. "I'm feeling a little bit judged here, Zo."

"No judgment intended." She held up her hands. "But if that's how you really felt about Quinn, I understand the loss you must feel. But at least you two are still—"

"Friends?" He laughed bitterly, draining his beer. "Right. Because I can call her up and say, 'Hey, let's spend the weekend at my place in Charleston,' and Max would be totally okay with that," he said sarcastically, his brows drawn together.

"Right." Zora nodded. "And now that Dal and I are married, you feel like you've lost your two closest friends all at once." She sighed softly. "I get it."

"I doubt it," he said.

"No, I do," Zora insisted. "It's kind of how I felt whenever Dallas would get involved with someone else. They were suddenly taking up this space in his life that had always belonged to me. And they, of course, felt threatened by our friendship."

"Since you two are married now and planning on having your own little brood, I'm pretty sure the feel-

ings of his ex-girlfriends were pretty damn justified."
Cole smirked as he rinsed his bottle out in the sink. He
dropped it in the recycling bin.

"Point taken." Zora grinned. "Guess I owe them an
apology."

"And I owe you and Dallas one." Cole placed a hand
on her shoulder. "I have been an ass ever since you two
got back from Vegas, and I'm genuinely sorry, ZoZo."

He hugged her, and she sank into the warmth of her
brother's embrace, grateful that they'd called a truce.
Until Savannah, Sloane, Kayleigh and Quinn had come
into her life via her brothers and cousin, she hadn't had
many female friendships. And she and Cole had formed
a bond early on. So aside from Dallas, he'd always been
her next closest friend.

Zora could understand the pain her brother must be
feeling. Everyone else in his life seemed to be moving
on, leaving him behind. Which must've added to the
isolation of being the only member of their family not
involved in running King's Finest.

"We good?" he asked, letting her go and tweaking
the high topknot she'd pulled her hair into.

Zora slapped his hand away and patted her hair back
into place. "You know better than to touch a Black
woman's hair."

"Bet you ain't tellin' ol' boy that." Cole raised an
eyebrow and chuckled.

"Shut up." She poked her brother, her cheeks hot as
she thought about the way Dallas had first taken down
her hair and run his fingers through it. Zora pulled another beer out of the fridge and handed it to her brother.
"Now that we're friends again… I do have a confession
to make. Can we talk upstairs?"

Cole nodded, his expression laced with concern. "Of course. Let's go."

They went to the sitting room upstairs and settled on the couch.

Zora told her brother the truth. About her and Dallas's wedding in Vegas. About her decision to have a child on her own. And that she now realized that she was in love with her best friend.

Her brother listened patiently. Then he reassured her that their secret was safe with him before giving her a final word of advice.

"You're an Abbott, Zo. If I'm being honest, you're the toughest and most determined one of all of us. So are you going to hang around here pouting about missing Dallas, or are you going to find a way to make this work? Like you said, Dal is a good guy. Plus, he gets you. Let's face it, you might never find a combo like that again." He smirked.

"Very funny," Zora said.

Cole chuckled, then sighed. "Seriously, Zo, the guy really loves you. Anybody can see that. Dallas has already proved how much he's willing to sacrifice for you. The question is, what are *you* willing to sacrifice to make this work?"

Zora laid her head on her brother's shoulder and sighed.

*That* was the question she needed to answer.

# Twenty-Four

Dallas parked the Range Rover Velar in the attached garage of the villa in Vogar, Iceland, where he'd been staying for the past few weeks. Both the car and the villa had been graciously provided by his host, Einar Austarsson.

The spacious villa was a forty-minute drive from the Austarsson factory in Reykjavik. The all-glass garden house, equipped with a hot tub, provided an impressive view of Keilir—a hyaloclastite mountain created during subglacial eruptions during the Ice Age. In the distance, he could see Snæfellsjökull—a 700,000-year-old glacier-capped stratovolcano.

Sitting in the hot tub and taking in such awe-inspiring scenery was a lovely way to end the day. Under normal circumstances, such natural beauty would spur countless ideas for new designs. But instead, he'd spent most of the time that he wasn't actively working on the project thinking of Zora.

Sometimes, he could still hear her voice in his head. Encouraging him. Being an adorable smartass. Finally admitting she loved him and wanted to be with him.

To say he missed Zora was an understatement. He'd agreed to move forward with this project and his residency here in Iceland. But he had no intention of giving up on their marriage.

Would it be a challenge to coordinate their busy schedules and demanding work lives so they could spend more time together and provide a stable home for any children they brought into the world? *Yes*.

Would it be worth whatever sacrifice that Herculean task required? *A thousand times yes*.

For now, he had to settle for video calls and text messages. But as long as Zora was willing to try to find a way to work all of this out, Dallas remained hopeful.

Dallas turned the knob and entered the house. He halted immediately, scanning the room. Two familiar scents lingered in the air. The first was his grandfather's five-alarm chili. The second was…

"Zora?"

There was no answer.

He walked into the quaint kitchen with its stunning black cooktop island. The style of the island and gold accents gave it the feel of an Old World piece of furniture. A huge Dutch oven simmered on the stove. He lifted the lid and inhaled.

*Definitely* his grandfather's chili.

Dallas replaced the lid and turned around, and his heart nearly leaped out of his chest. He swallowed hard and stared at the woman before him, but he couldn't open his mouth to speak.

He'd thought of Zora incessantly. Dreamed of her each night. Had his brain conjured her into existence?

"Zora," he said again finally, whispering her name.

"Yes, babe." She smiled, inching closer. Her voice trembling. "It's me."

"But I just spoke to you this morning. You…you were in Berlin on your business trip," he stammered.

"I was." Zora stepped closer, her grin deepening. "But I'm here now. With you. And baby, there is no place in this world I would rather be."

Dallas's heart overflowed with an amalgam of emotions: surprise, joy, relief. He regarded his beautiful wife, through the haze of emotion that blurred his vision. She was gorgeous with her hair worn in long, thick glossy twists, half of which were pulled up into a high topknot.

He closed the space between them, cradling Zora's face in his hands. Dallas pressed his mouth to hers, capturing her soft lips in a passionate kiss.

Zora wrapped her arms around him, her fingers clutching the fabric of his wool sweater.

He'd missed the comfort of her arms. The sweetness of her kiss. The contentment of being in her presence. And now that he held her in his arms again, he honestly didn't think he'd ever be able to let her go again.

Zora squealed when Dallas lifted her suddenly, sweeping her off of her feet and carrying her to his bedroom.

"The chili," she reminded him. "Your mom gave me your family recipe, and I don't want to screw it up."

"It'll be fine. It's on simmer," he muttered, carrying

her to the bedroom where he'd slept alone every night for the past few weeks. Wishing she was there.

Dallas made love to his wife, determined to make up for every moment they'd missed. Hoping he could convince her to stay.

Dallas lay in bed holding Zora in his arms, her cheek pressed to his chest. He'd left her just long enough to slip on his underwear and pad across the heated floors to turn off the chili.

"Zora, you have no idea how much I've missed you." He kissed her forehead, damp with perspiration.

"I think I do." Zora raised her head. Her espresso-brown eyes sparkled, and the smile on her face made his heart dance. "I missed you, too. *Desperately.*"

"How long can you stay?" He twirled one of the loose twists around his finger. "Hopefully until my flight home for Thanksgiving."

"Yes." Zora was barely able to contain her grin. "And if you don't mind having a roommate, I plan to return here with you after Thanksgiving. I'll make this my base until your project ends."

"You're kidding?" His heart beat wildly in his chest. "How? I mean…what about your bid to be CEO?" He sat up with his back against the headboard.

Zora sat up too, pulling the blankets up around her. "We all agreed that Blake should be KFD's next CEO."

"And you're okay with the decision?"

"I am. At this point in my life, the prospect of running the company doesn't give me the kind of joy and fulfillment I'd always imagined it would."

"What would?" Dallas asked, stroking her cheek.

"Being a wife and a mother." Zora smiled softly. "But

also spearheading the creation of KFD's new charitable foundation. There are so many projects and causes I'm passionate about. So much good we could be doing in the world. While I'm here with you, I'll work on making that happen."

"That's wonderful, Zora. But you didn't do this just because—"

"My family has discussed starting a foundation a few times over the years. No one took up the cause, so we always kicked the can down the road. Now feels like the right time for me to do this. And yes, it would give me more flexibility while our children are young."

A huge grin slid across Dallas's face.

"What is it?" Zora asked, smiling, too.

"You said our *children*. Does that mean—"

"That I love you, and that I want to be your wife forever and ever?" She smiled, tears streaking down her face. "Yes, Dal, it does."

"Then there's one more thing I need to do." Dallas slid to the floor on one knee and took Zora's hand in his. His mouth was suddenly dry and there was a fluttering in his gut.

"I apparently said this before." He chuckled. "But I need to say it again, because I don't ever want you to doubt it." Dallas drew in a shaky breath and his smile widened. His eyes welled with emotion.

"I love you, Zora Abbott. I have since the day I first met you on that playground. You've been in my corner since we were six years old. I loved you then, and I love you now. I have been waiting for this moment my entire life. I want to spend the rest of my life being your best friend, your lover, and the father of our children." His voice broke slightly. "Please say that you'll *stay* my wife forever."

Salty tears spilled down Zora's cheeks as she bit her lower lip and nodded, "Yes, Dallas. Nothing in the world would make me happier than to spend the rest of my life with you."

# Epilogue

Dallas lay in the bed he and Zora now shared in Vogar, Iceland. They'd returned home to Magnolia Lake to spend Thanksgiving with their families. Much to his surprise, Zora and their mothers had planned a simple but elegant wedding ceremony for their families that Saturday. They'd returned to Iceland a week later after a proper honeymoon in Costa Rica.

They would board their flight back to Magnolia Lake for the holidays tomorrow morning. Dallas was content to lie in bed with his wife, her warm, soft body melded to his as they lay together naked.

Zora kissed his bare chest, then lifted her head. Her hair, which she now wore in loose curls, was wild because he'd run his fingers through it when he'd made love to her. Her hair partially covered her face. But he couldn't miss her smile. His wife practically glowed with happiness.

"I got you an early Christmas gift." He suddenly remembered the gift-wrapped package he'd picked up in Reykjavik earlier that day.

Zora grinned. "I've got something for you, too."

Dallas climbed out of the bed to go find his bag and retrieve the gift. He presented it to her, and she opened the prettily wrapped box with its shiny, gold ribbon, pulling the merino wool sweater dress out of the box and grinning.

"I love it. It's gorgeous." She beamed, thanking him as she leaned over to kiss him. Then she retrieved a small box from the drawer of the bedside table and handed it to him. "Here's yours."

Dallas loosened the ribbon that tied the box and opened it. He stared at his gift. His eyes widened and his heart thudded in his chest. For a moment, he was unable to speak. He stared at the little white and blue stick with a single word on its digital screen: *Pregnant*.

"Is this…are we…"

"Yes." Zora laughed softly, placing a hand on her belly. "We're pregnant."

Dallas's heart raced and he couldn't stop smiling. He took his wife in his arms and hugged her.

"How long have you known?"

"I suspected as much last week, so I took a few different tests. I visited an OB/GYN earlier today. She confirmed it," Zora said. "You are happy about this, aren't you? Because I am hopelessly in love with you, Dallas Hamilton. And I can't wait to raise this baby with you. You're not only my best friend, you're the love of my life." Her eyes were wet with tears.

"I love you so much, Zo. And I could not be happier."

He leaned down and kissed her belly, then pressed another to her lips.

Dallas had been granted everything he could've ever wished for. He could receive no greater gift. And it was worth whatever sacrifices they'd have to make to build a life together.

\* \* \* \* \*

*If you enjoyed Zora and Dallas's story,*
*discover the blast from the past who reforms*
*bad boy Cole Abbott and steals his heart,*
*as Reese Ryan's series*
*The Bourbon Brothers*
*concludes in November 2021.*

*Available from Harlequin Desire.*

COMING NEXT MONTH FROM

# ⊞HARLEQUIN

# DESIRE

## Available April 13, 2021

## #2797 THE MARRIAGE HE DEMANDS
*Westmoreland Legacy: The Outlaws* by Brenda Jackson
Wealthy Alaskan Cash Outlaw has inherited a ranch and needs land owned by beautiful, determined Brianna Banks. She'll sign it over with one condition: Cash fathering the child she desperately wants. But he won't be an absentee father and makes his own demand...

## #2798 BLUE COLLAR BILLIONAIRE
*Texas Cattleman's Club: Heir Apparent* • by Karen Booth
After heartbreak, socialite Lexi Alderidge must focus on her career, not another relationship. But she makes an exception for the rugged worker at her family's construction site, Jack Bowden. Sparks fly, but is he the man she's assumed he is?

## #2799 CONSEQUENCES OF PASSION
*Locketts of Tuxedo Park* • by Yahrah St. John
Heir to a football dynasty, playboy Roman Lockett is used to getting what he wants, but one passionate night with Shantel Wilson changes everything. Overwhelmed by his feelings, he tries to forget her—until he learns she's pregnant. Now he vows to claim his child...

## #2800 TWIN GAMES IN MUSIC CITY
*Dynasties: Beaumont Bay* • by Jules Bennett
When music producer Will Sutherland signs country's biggest star, Hannah Banks, their mutual attraction is way too hot...so she switches with her twin to avoid him. But Will isn't one to play games...or let a scheming business rival ruin everything...

## #2801 SIX NIGHTS OF SEDUCTION
by Maureen Child
CEO Noah Graystone cares about business and nothing else. Tired of being taken for granted, assistant Tessa Parker puts in her notice—but not before one last business trip with no-strings seduction on the schedule. Can their six hot nights turn into forever?

## #2802 SO RIGHT...WITH MR. WRONG
*The Serenghetti Brothers* • by Anna DePalo
Independent fashion designer Mia Serenghetti needs the help of Damian Musil—son of the family that has been feuding with hers for years. But when one hot kiss leads to a passion neither expected, what will become of these star-crossed lovers?

YOU CAN FIND MORE INFORMATION ON UPCOMING HARLEQUIN TITLES,
FREE EXCERPTS AND MORE AT HARLEQUIN.COM.

HDCNM0321

SPECIAL EXCERPT FROM

**HARLEQUIN**

# DESIRE

*Wealthy Alaskan Cash Outlaw has inherited a ranch and needs land owned by beautiful, determined Brianna Banks. She'll sign it over under one condition: Cash fathering the child she desperately wants. But he won't be an absentee father and makes his own demand...*

*Read on for a sneak peek at*
The Marriage He Demands
*by* New York Times *bestselling author Brenda Jackson.*

"Are you really going to sell the Blazing Frontier without even taking the time to look at it? It's a beautiful place."

"I'm sure it is, but I have no need of a ranch, dude or otherwise."

"I think you're making a mistake, Cash."

Cash lifted a brow. Normally, he didn't care what any person, man or woman, thought about any decision he made, but for some reason what she thought mattered.

It shouldn't.

What he should do was thank her for joining him for lunch, and tell her not to walk back to Cavanaugh's office with him, although he knew both their cars were parked there. In other words, he should put as much distance between them as possible.

*I can't.*

Maybe it was the way her luscious mouth tightened when she was not happy about something. He'd picked up on it twice now. Lord help him but he didn't want to see it a third time. He'd rather see her smile, lick an ice cream cone or... lick him.

HDEXP0321

He quickly forced the last image from his mind, but not before a hum of lust shot through his veins. There had to be a reason he was so attracted to her. Maybe he could blame it on the Biggins deal Garth had closed just months before he'd gotten engaged to Regan. That had taken working endless days and nights, and for the past year Cash's social life had been practically nonexistent.

On the other hand, even without the Biggins deal as an excuse, there was strong sexual chemistry radiating between them. He felt it but honestly wasn't sure that even at twenty-seven she recognized it for what it was.

That was intriguing, to the point that he was tempted to hang around Black Crow another day. Besides, he was a businessman, and no businessman would sell or buy anything without checking it out first. He was letting his personal emotions around Ellen cloud what was usually a very sound business mind.

"You are right, Brianna. I would be making a mistake if I didn't at least see the ranch before selling it. Is now a good time?"

The huge smile that spread across her face was priceless… and mesmerizing. When was the last time a woman, any woman, had this kind of effect on him? When he felt spellbound? He concluded that never had a woman captivated him like Brianna Banks was doing.

*Don't miss what happens next in*
The Marriage He Demands
*by Brenda Jackson, the next book in her*
*Westmoreland Legacy: The Outlaws series!*

*Available April 2021 wherever*
*Harlequin Desire books and ebooks are sold.*

Harlequin.com

HDEXP0321

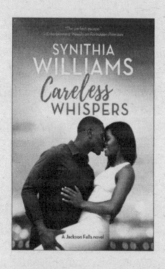

## SPECIAL EXCERPT FROM

HQN

*Return to Jackson Falls for the next sexy and irresistible book in Synithia Williams's reader-favorite series featuring the Robidoux family!*

*When everything is working to keep them apart, can these two former enemies learn to trust one another for a chance at forever?*

*Read on for a sneak peek at*
Careless Whispers

She turned to face him, her heart pounding again and a dozen warning bells going off in her head. She should shut down the flirting, but the look in Alex's eyes said he was willing to go with her down this path. "I've got some experience with wanting the wrong man."

"But that's all in your past now." He took a half step closer.

She shook her head. She'd never been good at not going for what she wanted. Her ego needed stroking, and Alex with his quiet understanding and empathy had shown her more care than anyone had in a long time. She'd be smarter this time. This was just to quell her curiosity. People said there was a thin line between love and hate. Maybe all their bickering had just been leading to this.

"Not quite," she said, choosing her next words carefully. She pretended to check the list in her box. "I find myself thinking about someone who I once despised. I miss clashing with him daily. I enjoy the verbal sparring. Not to mention he recently wrapped his arms around me, and for some reason I can't get that out of my head." She glanced at him. "He's stronger than I imagined. His embrace comforting in a way I didn't realize I'd like. It makes me want more even though I know I shouldn't."

Alex stilled next to her. "What are you going to do about this ill-advised craving?"

"It kind of depends on him," she said. "I think he's interested, but I can't be sure. And you know I can never offer myself to a man who didn't want me." She said the last part with a slight shrug. Though her heart imitated a hummingbird flitting against her ribs, and a mixture of excitement and adrenaline flowed with each beat.

Alex slid closer, closing the distance between them and filling her senses with him. He pulled the paper out of her hands. "What if he wants you, too?"

His deep voice slid over her like warm satin. She faced him and met his dark eyes. "Then I'm in trouble, because I'm no good at saying no to the things I want but shouldn't have."

*Don't miss what happens next in...*
Careless Whispers *by Synithia Williams.*

*Available March 2021 wherever*
*HQN books and ebooks are sold.*

HQNBooks.com